RANGER

HEARTLANDS MC

FRANKIE LOVE

ABOUT

RANGER: HEARTLANDS MC

When I find Ruby stranded, abandoned, and terrified, I know this innocent woman belongs with me.
I spent years in the trenches but now I'm home, in the Heartlands, and I'm ready to put down roots with this girl I never knew I needed.
Even though Ruby's a preacher's daughter, she's lost her faith in love.
When my worst fear comes to pass, it's my duty to prove to her that true love conquers all.
I will find her, whatever the cost.
She may be lost, but by God, she will be found.

Dear Reader,
Ranger's devotion to Ruby is no exception.
He will love her hard, love her deep, love her forever.
And then they'll ride off into the sunset... while stopping for a few quickies along the way!
xo, frankie

*The alpha males of Heartlands Motorcycle Club are **the most possessive, devoted, and territorial men** in the country when it comes to the ones they love.*

Heartlands is a rough and rugged new series of standalone stories. Written by four of the most trusted names in short and steamy romance, each book will get your motors revved and your hearts racing. Guaranteed.

XO, Frankie, Dani, Olivia, and Hope

1

RANGER

THE SUN IS JUST BEGINNING to set, purples and pinks cross the sky like a painting. As I ride down the highway, I can't help but thank God for this sense of freedom. A freedom I fought for as an Army Ranger.

Now I'm home, back in the heart of America, living the goddamn dream — the Road Captain for Heartlands Motorcycle Club, working on bikes down at the garage by day and running Ride or Die — our bar — by night. Always thanking my lucky stars that I made it out of the war zone alive.

Sure, my heart was pretty fucking bruised after seeing what I saw, but nothing was broken. Nothing shattered. Here I am, in one piece. Can't say as much for some of the Rangers I stood with.

It makes my commitment to *this* brotherhood all the stronger. All the more real. I know what it means to make a sacrifice — I've seen it. And I am committed to doing what it takes to protect the ones I love.

I grip the handlebars, accelerating as I ride down

the open stretch of highway, wheat fields to my left and right. I pass the Johnsons' big red barn and pickup trucks zoom past loaded with bales of hay.

As I wind my way toward my exit, I see a shitty two-door car with the hood up, smoke everywhere, on the side of the road. A woman is pacing, hands wrapped around her curvy waist.

Pulling over, I get off my Electra Glide and run a hand over my beard. It's the middle of summer, but as the wind sweeps over the fields around us, I look up to the sky — a storm is brewing. Turning that pink and purple sunset into a witch's cauldron.

"You okay, ma'am?" I say, her back toward me. What I see though is curves covered in a simple pale blue sundress, long wavy blonde hair down her back, sandals on her feet, and a petite frame that makes my cock twitch.

She turns, eyes brimming with tears, and she looks like an angel standing there on the side of the road, lit up by the sunset, illuminated as the clouds begin to roll in. I step toward her, knowing she is in need of something, desperate for it. I feel that from her even though I'm a few feet away.

She looks me over, and I see fear burning in her eyes. I understand. I know that my presence makes some people uneasy. I'm tall, with broad shoulders and muscles pulling at the seams of my white tee shirt. I'm a good foot taller than her, with a thick beard and tattoos running over my veins telling stories a sweet thing like her might not want to hear.

Still, I move closer. This car is smoking real bad and

she needs to get out of the way. "What happened here?" I ask.

"It started smoking, shaking, but I thought the car was drivable. It had been sitting out in the yard for months but... I think it's busted and..."

"Shit," I say, noticing the oil dripping from a cracked block and gas spouting from a busted fuel line. The damn thing must have shaken itself half to death. This thing is about to blow. I grab her, knowing it might seem rough, but my heart pounds as the engine roars with a last-ditch effort. The exhaust pipe fumes and pistons are fighting for life.

I pull her to the ground by my bike, covering her with my body as a massive burst of fire overtakes the tiny car.

"Oh my!" she cries, eyes blazing with fear. She trembles under me, and I move, lifting her body from the ground, making sure we are out of harm's way. "My life was in that car," she says, shaking as I pull her to my chest, scared she might do something stupid — run back for something that can't be saved.

"You'll be okay," I tell her. "You're safe — that's what matters."

She shakes her head, looking up at me. "No, I'm not," she says, wiping her eyes. "I was running away."

I search her face, wanting to understand, but the storm clouds break, and rain begins to fall. I need to get home — the worse the storm gets, the dumber it will be to be out in it on my bike. "We gotta make a break for it."

She swallows, looking back at the car, then up at me. "I don't even know your name."

"That's what you're worried about?" I ask as lightning slices the black sky.

I don't wait for a response. Taking her by the hand, I lead her to my bike. Grabbing my helmet, I buckle it under her chin. She doesn't look happy, but she doesn't resist, either. There's nothing but a barn two miles away, and beyond that, nothing but wheat fields and highway. I was out scouting routes for a possible club run.

She doesn't have much of a choice. If she had money, an ID, a bag — but it's all long gone, up in a fiery furnace. I'm her only hope and she knows it.

I get on my bike and tell her to jump on and hold tight. She does as I ask, her hands wrapping around my waist, squeezing so tight that I almost laugh. But then she whispers, "I've never been on a motorcycle before."

And I understand her vise-like grip. She's terrified.

I grip my handlebars, accelerating hard. Wanting to get this girl with golden hair and storm blue eyes and fragile heart — beating hard, so damn hard — home.

And for some inexplicable reason that I'm chalking up to it having been a long ass day, instead of asking where she wants to be dropped off, I head straight to my place, not once looking back at her car that minutes ago was engulfed in flames.

2

RUBY

NOTHING ABOUT TODAY is going how I planned. This great escape of mine is turning out to be a disaster. I ran to get away from Slider... but now I'm on the back of a motorcycle, holding onto a stranger's body. Wondering where I am supposed to go from here.

I'm more alone than I have ever been in my life.

Tears fall down my cheeks, and I squeeze my eyes shut, wind whipping against me as the sunshiny day turns to a reckless night wrapped up in rain, thunder. Lightning cracks through the deep sea-colored sky.

Not that I've ever seen a sea like that — not in real life, at least. I've seen pictures in books — but I've never travelled far from home, from my father's homestead. Communing with the congregation he led was my only connection with the outside world.

Now though, I long for an ocean I've never swam in, wanting to get swept away in a tide that would carry me away somewhere, far, far from here.

But as this man drives his bike off the exit toward a

big building set among oak trees and fields of hay, his voice, a low timbre, washes over me. "It's gonna be okay. I'll make sure of it."

I wonder if he is my ocean. If this stranger is both my deep-sea dive and my life raft. He rescued me, and now he is promising me that everything is going to be okay. My body shakes as he parks his bike, not knowing what comes next, but not wanting to be alone. Because I have no one else in this world who can help me. Lydia, though she'd want to, can't come to my rescue. I'm supposed to be the one setting up a new life in a city big enough to get lost in. Once I'm settled, I'll come for her.

But my little sister is going to be okay for now — Father isn't sentencing her to a life with a man like Slider. She is still only sixteen. She has some time. But me, I'm supposed to get married, the wedding set in a few days. I couldn't stay.

The parking lot is filled with motorcycles. Men huddle in circles under the covered awning, wearing leather and worn denim, smoking cigarettes. There are women with them dressed in short skits and high heels, their clothes accentuating their beauty. I feel small all of a sudden. He's brought me to a place as far from home as I can imagine, even though it's only a few hours' drive from where I've lived all my life.

The stranger helps me off the bike, and I realize he is handsome. Incredibly handsome, with deep eyes and strong hands, and muscles *everywhere*. I was preoccupied when he got me away from the fire, and I hadn't looked at him properly. I want to keep looking up at him, looking him over, but we can't stand here in the parking lot — the rain is pouring down on us, soaking through my flimsy dress, his white tee shirt drenched. Water falls down my cheeks as he unbuckles my helmet, storing it away. He takes his helmet off too, and the rain keeps pouring down.

He pulls me into the building. A bar.

I draw in a sharp breath, scared. He takes my hand, turning to me. "You look like you've seen a ghost."

I shake my head, droplets of rain falling to the floorboards. It's a dark room. Music plays and the bar is packed, customers sitting on stools. "I've never been in a bar before."

He frowns, leaning in. "How old are you?"

"Twenty-one." Then I smile, despite the trepidation surrounding the day. "I just had my birthday."

He gives me a soft smile then, an eyebrow lifting. "That so?" Someone hollers and he raises a hand. "Gimme a sec?"

I swallow, scared to be left alone, and he must realize this. My dress is soaked though, clinging to my skin. My hair is wet — I'm sure I look like a drowned rat. And I've never felt so out of place in my life.

"It's okay, I won't leave you," he says, as if reading my thoughts.

"Thank you," I whisper as he takes my hand. The simple comfort in it reaches my heart, and I suck in a deep breath as his fingers wrap around mine, enveloping me in a way I need so badly. It's like his hand around mine is the safety net pulling me from the watery depths. Saving me.

I follow, wordlessly, and as he leans over the bar, he lets go of my hand. I wish I was brave enough to reach for his, but I know the thought is insane. I don't know this man at all. As he speaks to a bartender, I keep my head down, eyes low. Like I've been taught to do all my life.

I feel people staring, but only a few men walk over to us.

A man who has arms covered in tattoos takes us in. "You all right, Ranger?" He claps my rescuer on the shoulder. *Ranger.*

"Yeah, got caught in the rainstorm." Ranger looks over at me. "Car trouble — she needed a ride."

"Going for a long ride to Hell's Landing tomorrow — you in?" another man asks.

Ranger shrugs, not giving him a straight answer. "We'll see. If the weather shapes up, that'll be a nice ride." Ranger takes two bottles of beer from the bartender, then slips a hand onto the small of my back. "We're gonna go upstairs to my place. She needs to make some calls where it's quieter."

The men nod, walking away, and I wonder where this is going... I want to believe Ranger isn't going to hurt me... but I haven't exactly known any men with pure intentions. And this man, this place, they're the epitome of what my father has preached against. Alcohol, tattoos, cigarettes. And even though I'm in the devil's playground, so long as I'm next to Ranger, I don't feel scared.

As Ranger takes me outside at the back of the bar

and leads me up a flight of stairs to a second-floor door, I exhale a sigh of relief.

I may not have any idea where this man is taking me, what he plans to do with me, but anything is better than marrying Slider.

3

RANGER

SHE'S SHAKING like a bird and I don't know if it's because she's scared or if she's cold. When I open my apartment door, I realize I kept the windows open, and I immediately move around the studio, shutting them to keep the rain out. She doesn't hesitate to help. She reaches for a window over the kitchen sink and closes it quickly. Seeing her bent over in a dress sticking to her skin, my cock twitches. Damn, she looks good. Then she turns, meeting my eyes as she reaches for the window next to the couch. I try not to smile, but I know she caught me.

"Thanks," I say, offering her one of the beers. She shakes her head no as I wipe my brow. "You sure?"

"I've never drank," she says, then bites down on her pink bottom lip.

"Right," I say, setting the extra Bud Light on the counter. "Shit, I shouldn't have assumed. Do you need to make a call now that we're out of the rain? Hell, I can get you a taxi." I shrug. "There are always half a dozen down at the bar taking home people who are drunk off their asses."

She flinches at my words and again, I'm left guessing. Was it my swearing or was it her not wanting to make a call?

"I can imagine how this is going to sound but... do you know if there are any women's shelters in the city? My wallet was in the car, and everything I owned. I don't know anyone I can call, and I don't have anyone I can..." She covers her face then, and I realize wherever she was headed before I found her was far, far away. She had plans to leave wherever she came from and then her car broke down and whatever she set out to do, she was stopped in her tracks.

"Hey, hey there — you're okay," I say, not knowing if that's the truth. "Long as you're with me, you're safe."

She sobs against my chest as I wrap her in my arms, not knowing what else to do. And I must admit I like having her there, pressed against me. She's soft and warm, and I like the idea of taking care of her. Not just because she is a woman in need — but because this woman in need makes my heart fucking pound in a way no one else in the world ever has.

"You're not going to some shelter in Seneca. You'd be eaten alive. Besides, it's safer here." I know the guys I ride with have a reputation – hell, we all do – but we're cleaning up our act. The club president, Troy Conley, is seeing to it. Still, I know what the headlines say. Saint, our Sergeant of Arms, is in prison right now on account of murder.

But I'm hoping this sweet thing doesn't know that.

Besides, she is safest here with us. We may look mean, but we never hurt our own.

She looks up at me, her thin dress making it hard for me to focus. Damn, she's beautiful. "It was a miracle, you coming for me when you did. I would have been out in that storm if you hadn't come…" A tear falls down her cheek and I brush it away with my thumb.

"What's your name?"

She licks her lips. "Ruby," she says.

"I'm Ranger."

She nods. "Your friends down there, are they as kind as you?"

I smile softly. "I don't know about that." I brush a strand of hair from her face. "You can stay here tonight," I tell her.

She nods, looking around my place. It's small, but respectable.

"I live alone and don't need much," I tell her, wondering what she thinks of my simple space.

She nods, taking deep breaths. "Thank you for giving me a place to sleep. I feel like you're my guardian angel or something."

I smile. "You're the one who looked like an angel when I first saw you today."

Her eyebrows lift. "You thought that?" She shakes her head, cheeks pink. "I'm no angel," she says.

I want to ask why she'd say that, but I know it's not really my business. My duty right now is to get her warmed up. "The bathroom is right over here," I tell her. "A shower will probably feel good. And I can find you something to wear."

She nods. "Okay, thanks, Ranger."

My name on her lips sounds so right. I force myself to walk away though and push open the bathroom door. "Towels are here, and I bet you're hungry. I'll get you some food, okay? I'll just be down at the bar for a second getting us dinner, okay?"

She bites her lip again. "You sure no one will come up here?"

"I'm sure. I'll even lock the door, okay?"

She nods and steps into the bathroom, closing the door. I hear the lock set and I exhale, dropping my shoulders, wondering what in the world I've gotten myself into.

I change quickly, then set a pair of sweats and a sweatshirt outside the bathroom door. Then I lock the apartment door and take the steps two at a time, telling Bulldog, our bouncer, to watch and make sure no one goes up the stairs to my place. Bulldog's bark is meaner than his bite, and his knuckle tats sum him up: LOVE HARD. I wonder when the bastard will find a woman to love the way he wants.

"Sure thing, Boss," he tells me as I step inside the bar I manage. Pulling open the door to the kitchen, I tell my line cook, T-Bone, I want a few cheeseburgers and fries, and I grab a few Cokes from the case.

"I have someone else's order done now. You want that?" T-Bone asks and I nod. He's a good man, grey haired and old enough to be my grandpa and always looking out for the girls, Roxanne and Stella, who work here. Means a lot. He puts the food in to-go boxes and stacks them one on top of the other. "Need anything else?"

"This is good, thanks," I say, taking my food and then walking through the front of the bar to see if I can find Killian and Chain before I leave for the night.

I catch Killian's eye and he walks right over to me. "What's the deal?" he asks. As the club president's son, he wants to know before any shit hits the fan.

"I got Ruby upstairs and she's staying with me tonight."

He grins. "Oh, she's got a name now?"

"Fuck you," I say with a laugh.

"It's just funny, you taking a girl home."

"Why's that funny?" I ask, already knowing the answer.

"You've turned down every woman in this bar at least twice. Never sleep with a soul when we go on rides for the weekend. You're solo."

"It's not like that. Ruby was stranded — she needed help."

Killian laughs. "Okay, Ranger, whatever you wanna call it."

I grunt. He isn't wrong — Ruby is beautiful, and I've never been tempted by another woman because no other woman has been her. She's different. Soft in ways that my hard heart craves. Quiet in a way that makes my restless mind still. I've known her an hour and yet I would move heaven and earth to make sure she's in my bed tonight.

"I gotta go," I say, thinking of her all alone upstairs. I

trust Bulldog with my life, but maybe I don't quite trust him with hers.

I'm the only man who can truly protect her.

We may have just met, but I know that for certain.

4

RUBY

THE SHOWER IS HEAVENLY. I turn the hot water up as high as it can go and try not to think about Lydia. She knows my plan, but the tears in her eyes when we said goodbye are impossible to forget. My sister needs me to figure out a plan for us both.

I know nothing can be sorted tonight. Right now, I can just be grateful that Ranger showed up when he did... he seems trustworthy, and I have no other option but to hope for the best. Without a phone or wallet, stranded in an unfamiliar town, what other choice do I have?

And I can't deny the comfort I feel when I am in his presence. When he held me close as I cried, my pounding heart calmed — my fear subsided. I could take a deep breath and believe that my life wasn't over.

In fact, maybe it's just beginning.

I let the hot water wash my troubles away, rubbing soap over my skin before rinsing off.

Even though I have never been alone with a man in

his home before, I don't feel uncomfortable. From what I saw of Ranger's apartment, it is clean and cozy, and even if there is a raucous bar below, the insulation must be great because all I hear is a steady beat. I can't make out much else.

I dry off with a fluffy grey towel, wrapping it around myself before peeking out the bathroom door. Ranger isn't here, and I smile, seeing the clothing he set out for me. I take it back inside the bathroom and hold up the grey sweatpants. I laugh to myself, knowing there is no way they'll fit — they would fall right to my ankles.

The soft blue sweatshirt will work, though. I put it on, and it hangs to my mid-thigh. Stepping into his home without a bra on is one thing, but wearing no panties is another. I look around the bathroom, hoping for a hair dryer to quickly blow dry them, but he doesn't have one, which isn't much of a surprise considering his short hair.

Placing my sundress, bra, and panties on the shower rod to dry, I try to ignore the flush of immodesty that I am not just considering — but am going through with. I've got nothing underneath this sweatshirt. I grew up in the church and was taught all about the world being black and white, but in my heart, I always felt there was a whole lot more grey than my father would acknowledge.

Being here in Ranger's home, half-naked, doesn't feel wrong. It feels like I am taking a chance on myself. For the first time in my life. I just wish Lydia was here with me.

Not wanting to cry, I steel myself to be practical. I

find a comb and I run it through my hair. I part it down the middle and look at myself in the mirror. Being here in this apartment brings out a sense of freedom I've never experienced before. Like I could do anything. I already did the hardest part — leaving my father's house, forsaking the union he had planned for me. Maybe I can find freedom in other ways tonight, too.

There was no way I could marry Slider. No way I could give myself to man who saw me as a prize, not a person. But it doesn't mean I don't want to give myself to someone... I just want it to be a man I feel safe with, secure. I want to give my body to a man who won't use it against me, who won't hurt me.

Something stirs inside of me when I hear the front door open, hear Ranger call for me, telling me he is back. A longing deep in my core, a desire for more, offers me a sense of confidence I don't usually feel. And that longing is directed at one person. One man. Ranger.

I squeeze my eyes shut, knowing we just met and I've saved my virginity all my life. Still, as I step out of the bathroom, watching as Ranger's eyes run up my bare legs, my bare thighs, over my curvy hips and my breasts — nipples hard and poking against the cotton of the sweatshirt — and I swear he groans.

I swallow, stepping closer. He has containers of food in his hands and I smile, grateful for something to do besides stare at this handsome man with longing.

"You got us food?" I ask, my heart skipping, and I clench my pussy tight, fully aware of how wet I suddenly feel. How needy my pussy is growing just as I stand here with him. He can't take his eyes off of me.

And hour ago, I was straddling his motorcycle, and now I have this insane image of myself straddling him. It's nothing I've ever considered doing before, but suddenly I can't think of anything else.

"Yeah, cheeseburgers — that okay?" I must take too long answering because he steps closer to me, worry in his eyes. "You okay, Ruby? You look lost."

I shake my hair, droplets of water hitting the hardwood floor. "I'm good," I say. "Just starved, I guess."

He nods and sets the food on the kitchen table, turning on another overhead light. He pulls out a chair for me and I smile, appreciating the gesture. We sit opposite one another and begin to eat. He eats like a man, with intention, and I focus on my food, not the heat in my belly.

We eat in silence and it starts to spread too wide. For a moment, I wonder if I read this wrong — read him wrong. Maybe he wasn't looking at me with hunger at all. Maybe he was just literally *hungry*. And maybe these cheeseburgers took care of all his cravings.

"The shower okay?" he asks, eyes on his pile of fries.

I lift the can of Coke to my lips, answering with a quick yes before taking a sip.

"Good. I think I might head in for one myself, if that's okay with you?"

I nod. "Of course. This is your home."

"I spoke to Bulldog."

I frown, trying to follow.

"He's the bouncer downstairs. He knows to keep an

extra eye on the stairwell to my place. No one knows you're here."

"Your friends at the bar do," I say softly.

He nods. "Far enough. But they're bikers. We don't share with outsiders."

"Sounds... intense."

Ranger frowns. "These men — they're like my family."

I try not to scoff, but I can't help it.

"You have a problem with family?" he asks, wiping his hands on a towel.

"Just because someone is family doesn't mean you can trust them."

He pushes his container of food away. "You're running away from home and lost, so I get your lack of faith."

"I have faith."

"Yeah? What kind of faith do you have?" he asks, eyebrow raised, not giving me much room to get away from the answer. He is pushing me for my opinion and no man has ever once done that before — asked me what I thought on a matter. Any matter.

"I have faith in myself."

Ranger stands, dropping our trash in a bin. "Sounds about right." Then he turns to me. "But that seems kinda lonely, doesn't it? To be the only person you can trust?"

I swallow, wondering how he got to the heart of things — the heart of me — so quickly. I stand and reach for a rag to wash down the table. It's habit, taking care of the home. "I get lonely," I admit, running the cloth over the pine tabletop. "But there are worse things than feeling alone."

"Like what?" he asks. His voice is deep, gravelly, the timbre strong and solid.

I exhale the air I hadn't realized I was holding. "Like being scared."

Ranger steps closer behind me. His hands run over my wet hair, brushing it aside, and he whispers in my ear. "You aren't alone right now," he tells me, his hot breath sending a current down my spine. "But are you scared?"

"No." My voice is a whisper, tight but true.

He doesn't answer and I wonder if he believes that I feel brave. Alive. I want him to say more. I want his hands to move down my back, to spin me around and hold me again like he did when I cried. But this time, there won't be tears. There will just be longing.

But as I turn on my heelsw to face him, he is stepping back, toward the bathroom. "I'm going to shower now," he says, pulling the door shut before I can say another word.

And just like that, I'm left breathless. Left wanting. Left needing so much more.

5

RANGER

I STEP into the shower and do my best not to groan too damn loudly. Truth is, I had to step away because sitting across from Ruby was pure and absolute torture.

She is the most beautiful woman I've ever seen — I knew that the moment I picked her up on the side of the road, but freshly showered, in my sweatshirt, her tits perky, her hard nipples poking through — fuck me now because my cock is throbbing with desire.

I sat there eating my supper as best I could, and so long as we sat in silence, I was okay... but when she spoke, when her pretty pink lips parted, that sweet lull to her voice damn near had me coming then and there, my cock a steel rod aching to be pumped. Fuck, I want to fill her sweet pussy up in a way that leaves me dropping my head against the cold tiles of the shower.

She's more than an angel — she's a goddamn goddess. Whispering in her ear was a bad idea because now I want so much more. Yes, I told her she is safe with me, that she isn't alone — but I want to *show* her that. Prove that to her.

Actions speak louder than words, or so they say.

My cock aches and I'm tempted to stroke myself under the cold water, to get myself off, but it feels wrong somehow to pleasure myself to the thought of Ruby when she's standing right outside the door.

I urge my dick to calm the hell down and I finish showering, drying off and trying not to stare at her bra and panties hanging on the damn shower curtain rod.

Fuck.

If her panties are drying right there, that means they aren't on her cute little ass.

Which means her sweet pussy is bare.

My cock twitches, eager and losing all restraint. "Calm the hell down," I grunt.

"Did you say something?" Ruby calls from the apartment.

"No, it's all good," I say, just as I'm realizing I forgot clothes to change into. I wrap a towel around my waist and step out of the bathroom.

The moment I do, Ruby drops the glass of water she is holding. It falls to the floor, spilling all over, the glass shattering.

"Oh shoot," she says, starting to lean over, but I don't want her to deal with that after the day she's had, and besides, we're both barefoot.

"Don't move," I say, strutting over and picking it up myself. Then I reach for the broom.

As I do, my towel loosens and falls to the hardwood floor.

I chuckle, realizing things went from bad to worse... but when I look up and meet Ruby's eyes, I see desire swirling around her irises. Maybe I was wrong. Maybe things have just gone from good to great.

"Here, let me," she says, taking the broom from my hand as I pick up my towel. I take my sweet time, walking to the laundry hamper, dropping it in. There's a chance a piece of glass might have got caught in the threads.

I feel her eyes on my naked body, and look over my shoulder to check. Yep. She's zoomed in. I admit it, I flex my ass just because I can.

"I'll grab another towel, don't worry."

She shakes her head, cheeks turning bright red, her damp hair falling into her eyes. She brushes it aside. "You don't need to on my account. I mean... I think you look very... nice."

I grin, turning to her, cupping my junk with my hands. "Nice, huh? I suppose I oughta get another towel to cover up all this *niceness*."

She licks her lips, emptying the dustpan in the trash, setting the broom aside, and then she gets on her hands and knees, wiping away the water that was spilled.

Fuck, seeing her down there like that makes my cock twitch again, harder now. Longing. Desperate. I step toward her.

"There," she says. "All cleaned up." She looks up, eyes on my hands — hands that are attempting to cover my cock. "You don't need to get a towel if you don't want."

"No?" I say, wondering where this might lead.

"No. I mean... I..." She shakes her head. Flustered. "I don't know what I'm saying."

"It's okay," I say, taking her hand and helping her stand, staying decent with my other hand. "You don't have to know what you want."

She frowns, indignant. "Oh, I know what I want."

My mouth twitches, and I suppress a smile. Damn, this girl is adorable when she gets herself worked up. "You do?"

She shrugs. "I just don't really know how to ask for it."

"I'm surprised. I'd have guessed a woman as sweet as you always gets what she asks for."

She bites on her bottom lip. "No, that's not the way it worked with my father. With him, it was his way or the highway."

I lift the side of my mouth, resting my hand on her cheek. "That why I found you on the literal highway? You two have a fight?"

"Not a fight, Ranger. It was more than that." Her delicate eyes flare with something deep, burning. A fire. She's more than a sweet thing — she is a pillar of strength. "He wanted me to marry a man who is cruel. A man that doesn't respect women, doesn't respect me. That's why I left."

I nod slowly, taking her words in. "So, you don't have much experience asking for what you want... but it sounds like when you left today, there wasn't much discussion taking place. You just made up your mind and did the thing you wanted to do."

"You suggesting I do that now?" she asks. She runs her hands over her hair, breathing more softly now. Her nerves from seeing me naked have faded.

"You can do anything you like, Ruby. Like I said, you're safe here." Her eyes are cast down, but I lift her chin with the crook of my finger. "What is it you're scared of?"

"I'm scared of liking it all too much."

"Liking what?"

She exhales, reaching for my hand that is covering my cock. "Liking this." Her eyes linger on my thick shaft, and her breath shallows, her fingers inching toward my skin. "Liking that."

"Do you want to touch me, Ruby?" I ask, realizing that is what she is after. What she needs. A girl held back all her life, finally free. And I found her. How goddamn lucky am I?

"I want to do everything with you, Ranger."

I cup both her cheeks with my hands and her breath stills. "Have you ever been with a man, Ruby?"

She shakes her head. "No. I've never even kissed one."

I brush my thumb over her smooth skin. "Then let's start there."

I pull her to me, and she whimpers as our mouths press together, her lips soft and eager, parting as our tongues run over one another. I rest a hand on her waist, another on the base of her neck, and I kiss her with abandon, with the knowledge that this kiss right here is the first of her life — a kiss she will never, ever forget.

And neither will I.

She moans as I kiss her more deeply, and my cock throbs against her belly. Knowing she's got nothing under this oversized sweatshirt makes me ache with want. *I want to do everything with you.* Fuck, it's what I want too.

Bodies pressed together, I run a hand over her waist, to her ass, squeezing her cheeks. "That okay?" I ask between kisses.

"Do what you want to me."

"You don't want to be more specific?" I ask.

She shakes her head. "I know I want to feel something big. Something powerful. Something deep. But I don't know the words for that... that longing inside me."

"Where is that longing coming from?" I ask. Maybe it's her head, her heart — maybe it isn't about her physical needs.

But she steps back from our embrace, and lifts the hem of the sweatshirt, up past her belly. She presses her palm to her pussy, where a soft tuft of blonde hair covers her sweet virgin folds, tempting me more and more the longer I look.

"The longing comes from right here," she says, running her fingers over herself. "From inside here."

She dips her finger into her cunt and motherfucker, my cock is iron and there isn't much getting in our way, of her truly having everything she is talking about.

"Damn, Ruby, you're perfect."

I drop my head back, wondering how I won the goddamn lottery. Ruby is sweet and sincere and adorable and brave and here. Here with me, telling me she wants to do everything I can dream up.

"You haven't even seen all of me."

"I've seen enough to know you're the sexiest woman in the fucking world."

As if sensing my growing want, she pulls the sweatshirt off. "I mean it, Ranger. This is the most freedom I've ever experienced, and I want to enjoy it. Every last bit of it."

HE STEPS TOWARD ME, as if mesmerized by my body.

"God, Ruby," he growls.

"What?"

"Your tits — they're so sexy. Bigger than I expected, so fucking round now that they aren't hidden behind a bulky sweatshirt." He runs his hands over them, massaging them gently and making me whimper as he does. I've only been here for a few hours but already we have set aside all modesty and are offering one another our most vulnerable parts.

"Hell, these hips..." He shakes his head, whistles low. "There are the kind of hips a man can hold onto, the kind of hips that are made to be enjoyed."

"Then enjoy," I tell him, shaking at my boldness, but delighting in it all the same. This is the last way I expected this night to end — I was sure I'd pull over to a motel somewhere closer to the city, and lock the door, scared to fall asleep not knowing who might be prowling outside... but this... it's not the fear I thought I'd experience.

This is excitement. Anticipation. Knowing that Ranger has absolute reign over my body sends a thrill through me. Because with Slider, it was going to be him taking from me, whereas right now — this is on my terms.

And it's me giving, offering freely. It's me asking.

And that makes all the difference in the world.

Ranger must notice that my mind floated away for a moment. "You all right? We can slow down, we can stop altogether. Tell me what you need, baby. I'll give it to you."

I close my eyes, his words the sweetest sounds I've ever heard. A smile spreads across my lips and I want his hands to massage my breasts more. I want them cupped, touched, plucked.

He groans, dipping his mouth to my breast, sucking it, my nipple in his mouth, his tongue twirling around the hard nub, and I feel my core hot, wet, ready.

He lifts me from the floor and carries me to his bed, setting me down on the pillows, the comforter, the soft blanket cushioning my body. He moves on top of me, his hands warming my body, and every inch of me prickles with pleasure.

"I want to touch you. Can you show me what you like?" I ask him, looking up into his deep hazel eyes.

He nods, not laughing at my innocence, not belittling my lack of experience. Instead, he takes my fingers and gently wraps them around his big, thick cock. I can't reach my fingers all the way around him — he's too big. Too meaty, but also, so smooth. Like velvet. And my mouth waters as I stroke him softly, not wanting to hurt him. His balls look heavy and his thighs are muscular, his whole body resembling a chiseled piece of wood — strong and mighty and for tonight, mine.

It's hard to focus, so much is stirring within me all at once. "My pussy is so wet," I tell him. "Wetter than it was the one time I touched myself."

His fingers tease my nipples. He leans down, his mouth on my ear. "You touched yourself? Tell me."

Biting my bottom lip, I try to put words to the memory. "I'd been reading a book, one I found at the library. But I knew it wasn't one Father would like me to read. One I couldn't bring home. It was intimate…"

"How so?" he asks, his cock throbbing under my hand as I stroke him gently, realizing he is enjoying me recounting the time I explored my body. It's making him pleased, and right now, all I want to do is please Ranger — the man who saved me, who makes me feel safe, who makes me feel beautiful.

"Well, I took the book to the back reading area. It was late, and dark, and I was alone. In the book, the couple had sex. She let him come inside her. And I wanted to know what that felt like. I knew it was wrong, reckless even, but as I read, my pussy — it got so hot, almost painfully so. I needed to do something."

He runs his hand over my skin, past my belly, to my pussy, his fingers threading through my tufts of hair, to my folds.

I close my eyes, continuing my memory. "And I couldn't help it. With my back to the rest of the library, I pressed my hand under the waistband of my skirt, my panties, and I felt myself — the wetness, the heat..."

"Like this, Ruby? Did you touch yourself like this?" Ranger begins to explore my pussy with his fingers like I had... only better. Much better.

"Like that... yes. Everything started to seize up real tight and I didn't know what to do, and I got scared so I stopped."

He looks in my eyes. "So you didn't come? You didn't feel the orgasm in your toes, up your spine?"

I shake my head, feeling dizzy as he moves my hand from his cock, as he spreads my knees and begins to touch me with more intention.

"Relax," he tells me, leaning down to kiss my inner thighs, kissing me lower and lower, until his mouth, his beard, is fluttering over my pussy. Until his tongue is — oh!

"Can you do that?" I ask.

He lifts his head, smiling up at me. "Baby, I can do whatever I like, remember?"

I smile, remembering my request of him, and I let my head fall back, giving in to whatever this is. Knowing my father always preached that sex before marriage is against the Lord's will, but there is nothing more pure than what is happening right now. Ranger is erasing my fears, my pain, my heartache with his tongue, one sweet lick at a time. And each second that passes, my body heats up a little more, then a little more.

His tongue moves quickly, then slowly, and each change in speed makes my pussy ache even more. I moan loudly, unable to help myself. Gasping, I grip the bedsheets, wanting more. Wanting everything.

His fingers press against me. Moving quickly, until my knees are shaking, until my back arches and my breath is shallow. "What is this called?" I ask.

"A good old-fashioned finger fuck, Ruby." He laughs and so do I.

"That is the dirtiest thing I ever heard."

"But you like it, don't you?" he says, his hand stilling.

I nod vigorously. "Why did you stop?"

He grins, his smile so handsome, so utterly appealing that I drape my arm over my head, laughing as his mouth kisses my pussy again.

"And this is called going down on you," he says, informing me each step of the way. It's empowering and I'm glad he is telling me. "And this is called sucking your clit."

My eyes widen as he sucks on a nub of pleasure so intense I grip the sheets harder and begin to moan louder than I have ever imagined moaning in my life. "Oh my, oh, Rang — oh Rang — oh! Oh!"

His tongue flicks fast over me, then his fingers press back to my hole and what was wet before is now soaking. Gushing. My body feels split in two as his hand moves fast, faster, faster over my pussy, my moans turning to cries as he gets my body off in a way I didn't understand was possible.

"That's an orgasm, Ruby. That is your cute little cunt saying she's satisfied."

His words are shocking... and delightful.

I take a moment to catch my breath, realizing his blanket is soaked, my skin so hot. "So," I say, licking my lips and pulling him toward me, wanting to kiss those impossibly luscious lips again. "It wouldn't be fair if I was the only one satisfied, would it? Teach me, Ranger. How can I return the favor?"

SHE'S SWEETER than anything I've ever tasted in my life. My heart thrums to life as I get her off, moving my mouth over her dripping, tight hole. Loving the way she squirms in delight as I taste every last inch of her.

Once she comes hard against my mouth, my hands — there is no going back. When her lips part and she asks me to show her how to satisfy me the same way I've just satisfied her, my cock hardens to a steely rod.

"You feel how hard I am for you?" I ask her.

She strokes me tenderly. "I did that to you?"

I nod. "Yes, you. God, Ruby, you make me think crazy things. And we haven't even made love."

"What kind of things?" she asks, her hand stilling.

I run a hand over my beard, my other hand caressing her full tits. "You make me think finding you about to be caught in a storm was no coincidence."

Rain falls heavy on the tin roof, background music to the night of our lives. I want it to keep beating down, a blanket surrounding us, washing away our past, our mistakes, offering a fresh start. A clean slate.

"I need you, Ruby." It's not just my cock talking now — it's my heart too.

And she seems to understand because she wraps hers arms around my neck. Our lesson is forgotten because right now I don't feel like teaching. I just want to learn — learn all there is to know about her. And she feels it. I know she does. I lean over her, suckling her innocent tits, cradling her small frame in my arms, her legs wrapping around my body as my thick cock eases inside her sweet, creamy virgin cunt. She is so tight, so naïve, and my cock drums with desire, needing to come hard inside of her. My want is singular: I must mark her as my own.

"Oh, Rang," she moans as I begin to fill her up. "Don't stop, please. Never, ever stop."

"Does it hurt, baby?" I ask, not wanting to cause her any pain.

"No," she whispers as I pull her close to me. "It doesn't hurt like you'd think... it hurts in a way that feels good, in a way I need."

"I need it too," I tell her, my cock throbbing in her warmth. She is so tight, so innocent, so sure of what she wants.

I don't hold back. I take my time making sure every moment of this first time is beautiful. I want her to remember this night for the rest of her life. Remember it as tender and slow, as sweet and fucking hot.

She loves it, the way I pulse into her, excruciatingly slow, knowing the deep pleasure mounting in us both is something you can't fake, can't fabricate. You can't fake real and this is real. So fucking real it makes my cock explode so deep in her sweet little cunt that she is screaming my name as we come. As her body wraps around me, I swear to God she is holding on for dear life. We're drowning in one another. It's like we are lost at sea, but then, in one another's arms, we are found.

I won't let go.

Ever.

And as she gasps, finding her breath as her cunt is filled with my thick, milky seed, she laughs, delirious. Happy. She looks up at me, both satisfied and sleepy. Content.

"That was incredible," I tell her, leaning down and kissing her again, unable to help myself. I want to hold her all night — I won't let her go.

She seems to understand. We kiss until sleep demands an answer, and so we turn on our sides. I spoon her tightly, our hands held, her body nestled snug against mine, and I breathe her in. She smells like a summer rainstorm, like my favorite peppermint shampoo. She smells like a woman. My woman. Mine.

I fall asleep dreaming of a future with a woman whose past I barely know.

I dream of a life with this fragile stranger, who made her way into my arms, who sleeps pressed against my heart.

———

WE WAKE to bright streams of sunlight pouring through

the window. I run a hand over my beard, looking at the clock. Eyes widening. Holy shit. It's after nine a.m. I calculate how long we've slept... over eight hours. Straight.

I'm more well-rested than I've been in years.

I hardly ever sleep. Usually, I'm lucky if I get a few hours. Ever since I went to a war zone, I can't sleep too long without waking up. Remembering. I've worked through my shit, most of it at least — I mean, some things you can never unsee — but I'm stronger than I've been in a long ass time. Having my brothers in the Heartlands MC helps with that. When I get in a funk, they know to pull me out of it by going on a long ride to clear my head. It works every damn time.

But it's the lack of sleep that fucks with me.

Until last night.

Ruby snores softly and I smile, loving the way she looks when she's sleeping. So damn peaceful.

I get out of bed, needing to open a window — the heat is relentless in the summer, and I pull on a pair of shorts. I look out the window as I open it. Most of the cars are gone — the bikes too. I know from experience that the ones left are those of partiers who had one too many drinks last night and were taxied home at last call.

Ruby and I slept through all that — and I think about how different last night was from last weekend, how I'd been down at the bar pouring drinks when someone took a break, helping the line cook when he got slammed, keeping an eye on things in general. Up until four a.m.

Ruby seems to be stirring, so I make a pot of coffee, moving around as quietly as possible. I pull out a carton of eggs, scramble and cook them. Make toast. Preparing Ruby breakfast in bed. I find a cookie sheet and use it as a tray, carrying plates of food to the bed.

"Hey," she says, sitting up in bed and covering her chest with the sheets, smiling. "Look at all this. You can cook too?"

I grin. "So you're saying you think I have other skills?"

The sheet wrapped around her falls slightly as she reaches for the mug of coffee. As she lifts it to her mouth, she smiles. "I'd say you have a few other skills I can think of off the top of my head."

I get in bed with her, the cookie sheet resting between us, and I give her a soft kiss. "You know you snore?"

Her cheeks turn pink. "Lydia always reminded me of that."

"Who is she?"

She smiles softly, picking up a slice of toast. "My sister. She's five years younger than me — my best friend and the sweetest thing in the world."

"Sweeter than you?"

Ruby twists her lips. "Actually, she is equally sweet and feisty. She's still growing up though, figuring out who she is."

"And you, Ruby — you know who you are?"

Ruby sets down her toast. "I knew enough to know marrying Slider wasn't an option."

"Your dad really set you up to marry a guy you didn't love?"

She nods. "He was going to give my father's church a big check in exchange for my hand in marriage. My father was willing to sell me, basically. Me, his daughter."

"Where is you mom in all of this?"

"She died while giving birth to my sister." Ruby sips her coffee, looking out the open window. "What about your family? Where are they?"

"My family is ancient history. Dad left before I was born, Mom fought addiction all her life until it won the battle. By then I was eighteen, broken up about losing her, and so I left for the army. Became a Ranger and put in my time for eight years."

"Why'd you leave?"

I run a hand over my beard before picking up my coffee. "My unit went through hell. We were in Fallujah and shit hit the fan. Some of the guys didn't make it. Died in my goddamn arms. I was shot, too," I tell her, pressing her hand to the scar on my shoulder. "But I made it out alive, was honorably discharged after."

Ruby runs her fingers over my scar. "You've been through a lot," she whispers. "And yet here you are, still standing."

"We aren't standing right now." I take the tray and set it on the floor, then draw Ruby into my lap, kissing her softly, my cock loving it when she begins to stroke me, waking us both up. She dips her mouth to my cock, opening her lips and running her sweet tongue over my shaft.

"This okay?" she asks softly, her eyes dewy, her creamy ass lifted as she kneels before me.

"Fucking perfection," I growl as she begins to suck me the way I need. I love her innocent longing to please me, and my cock won't hide its true feelings. I'm so damn hard and horny for my girl and as she bobs her head up and down, there's no denying how I feel.

She is mine.

My hands run over her ass, and then I smile, knowing what her little pussy will like. I lift her knee and drape it over my torso so she's straddling me backwards. Lowering myself on the mattress, I draw her ass to my mouth and begin to suck her sweet hole the way she needs.

Moaning as she licks me up and down, fondling my balls as she deep throats my dick, I lick her cunt until my beard is tickling her nice and good. Her juicy folds weep as I dig my fingers into her cheeks, face-fucking my baby like she's my last goddamn meal.

"Ohh, ohh, ohhhh." She sucks hard as I shoot ribbons of come into her pink mouth, my cock rock solid as she sucks me off, my seed sliding down her throat as she drips against my mouth.

Breathless, she spins to me, facing me with a sultry pout. "You taste like salty cream."

I lift an eyebrow, her tits full, bouncy and ripe. "And?" My cock wants to come all over them too. But my sweet girl isn't ready for a dirty fuck like that. Not yet, at least.

"I loved the way it felt to have you in my mouth," she says, panting, tracing a line from my chest to my mouth. I grab her hand, suck her finger, our eyes locked. God, is it possible to start every damn day like this?

"Come here, baby," I say, needing her closer. Needing to fill her up again. I set her squarely in my lap, and she has her legs wrapped around me as she sinks down on my thick cock, her moaning growing loud as I fill her up nice and good.

"Oh Rang," she moans. "It feels so good," she breathes in my ear.

I run my fingers through her hair, holding her back, her big, bouncy tits pressed against my chest and her sweet cunt warm and wet. She bounces in my lap like a goddamn bunny and my cock throbs, ready to release.

"Fuck, baby," I groan as she digs her nails in my back, her orgasm running over her skin. "Oh, fuck yeah." We get off together and as we finish, I kiss her again, deeper now. Eventually, she rolls off my lap and leans over the bed. "What is it?"

"I think I need those eggs now. I officially worked up an appetite."

I bring the tray back up to the bed, chuckling. Just then, there is a loud knock on the door.

Her eyes widen, fear written on her face.

"Ranger," a voice calls from the other side of the door. "There's an emergency!"

8

RUBY

FEAR RUNS over my skin as Ranger walks to the door. I pull the sheet around me, bracing myself for something bad.

But when Ranger opens the door, the man in the doorway stands rigidly. Whatever he's about to tell Ranger isn't going to make him happy. "What's this about, Killian?" Ranger asks.

The man looking back at him, tattoos running over his arms and neck, is shaking his head. "The roof of the garage is busted through. The rainwater was too heavy, I think."

"Shit," Ranger says, grabbing his boots. He looks back at me. "I'll be back, okay? Just headed down to the garage on the other side of the parking lot."

"Okay," I say, nodding as he leaves. The moment he is gone, I get out of bed and carry the cookie tray to the kitchen table, sheet wrapped around me. I pour a second cup of coffee and then peek out the window, watching Ranger and Killian head to the garage.

There are a few men already there, pulling motorcycles and other equipment from the garage. But it's more of a mechanic's shop — the sign overhead reads HEARTLANDS GARAGE.

The men set to work quickly, opening up the big garage doors and working on getting the water out. They use tarps to patch the roof — I'm guessing a short-term solution to a bigger problem. But they are all working together, and there is something heart-warming about it, a group of men working on a common goal.

Wanting to be useful myself, I dress in the blue sundress — this time wearing my bra and panties — and slip on my sandals. I find a set of sheets in a cabinet, and make the bed fresh, then I do the dishes from breakfast, tidy up the studio, and braid my long hair, grateful there is a hair tie on my wrist because it's basically all I have to my name. Everything else went up in flames yesterday.

I look at Ranger's cellphone on the bedside table, tempted to call my sister, but I don't know his passcode. Besides, I don't want her to worry. I want her to hang onto hope for as long as possible. Calling her before I have a plan for us both won't do her any good. Besides, my father could very easily answer, and I don't know how easy it is to trace cellphones. But the last thing I want is Slider showing up here, forcing me to go home.

My heart is pounding just thinking about it — and I need fresh air. So, I step out of the apartment and walk across the parking lot to see the work the guys are doing up close.

The men Ranger spoke with at the bar last night give me a nod, and one of them shouts to him. "Your woman's here."

The words start a stirring in my heart, and I can't help but feel pride at the thought of being his woman.

Ranger jogs over to me and wraps me in his arms. "Hey, beautiful."

I smile up at him. "Everything going okay?"

He nods, giving me a kiss, not caring who in the world sees us. It's like he is staking his claim, his territory, and my whole body swells with emotion. I've never felt so good, so seen, so wanted in my life.

"Yeah, I have a buddy with a construction crew. They will be over later to patch the hole. And we have squeegees and mops for emptying the garage of the water. What a mess though, right?" We survey the scene and there are at least a dozen motorcycles in the parking lot, big toolboxes on wheels, and basically anything that could be dragged from the garage is drying in the sun.

"Thankfully 90 percent of the shit in there is metal."

I nod. "Need any help?"

"You could go in the bar and see if T-Bone, the line cook, needs any help. He's getting breakfast ready for everyone."

Biting my bottom lip, I betray how nervous I am to walk in there. Ranger must notice. "You'll be fine. He's nicer than he looks — promise." Then he pats my bottom and sends me on my way. I look back over my shoulder and smile. He is watching me walk away.

T-Bone gives me a big smile when I enter the

kitchen and there are a few other women with him. "Ranger sent me to help," I announce. "I'm Ruby."

"I'm Stella," a woman with long black hair says.

A woman with curly brown hair sticks out her hand for me to shake. "And I'm Roxanne. We bartend here. We're with the MC."

I frown. "The MC?"

Stella and Roxanne share a look. "Yeah, honey, the Heartlands Motorcycle Club? The crew your boy Ranger rides with?"

I nod, trying to catch up. "Truthfully, I don't know anything about MCs. I just met Ranger last night."

"Well, Ranger's the Road Captain," Stella says. "Means he organizes all the runs."

"I see," I say slowly, taking it in. "I didn't realize it was a whole organized club. I feel a little over my head, to be honest."

T-Bone grunts. "Sounds fancier than it is. Really just a bunch of men who are rough and rowdy."

"Hey," Roxanne frowns. "That's not true. Troy's cleaning us up."

Stella laughs. "Then what are you still doing around here?" The women laugh and my eyes widen, not in on their jokes.

T-Bone must sense my struggle because he hands me a package of bacon. "You know how to fry up some pork?"

"That is something I can handle." I may not know much about bars and bikes, but I do know how to cook. T-Bone notices and soon we are flipping flapjacks, scrambling dozens of eggs, and the whole kitchen smells like bacon.

"Look at you," he says, handing me a cup of coffee once the breakfast is finished. "I think you'll fit in here just fine."

Stella and Roxanne raise their eyebrows, though. T-Bone notices and laughs. "Don't be jealous just because you've wanted to sink your claws in Ranger for the last year."

Stella laughs, shrugging as she mixes a pitcher of bloody Marys. "Fair enough. I guess the best girl won."

"Oh, I didn't win anything. I just met him."

This time it's Roxanne who laughs. "Oh sweetheart, Ranger has never once taken a girl to bed in the time I've known him. If he slept with you, it means you won his heart, believe me."

Just then, the men from outside file in, talking loudly, grumbling about it being too damn early, then grinning as T-Bone and I carry platters of food to bar tables we've pushed together. Beers are poured and coffee is served, and we all sit down. I realize it's Sunday morning. But no one bows their heads. No one says grace.

Instead, the men dig into the food and as Ranger rests his hand on the small of my back, thanking me for helping with it, I realize this moment right here is what I've been praying for my whole entire life.

9

RANGER

THE NEXT FEW days pass in a blur. Not a bad blur — a good one. A blur of firsts as Ruby and I get to know one another on every level. She hands me wrenches as I lower myself under my bike. I stand outside the dressing room when I take her to the shopping center to buy herself some clothes. We make love in the shower, on the kitchen table, on the floor. We kiss until our lips are swollen and we fuck until she's got rug burn on her knees.

It's goddamn bliss.

When we wake up on the fourth day, I ask if she wants to go for a long ride.

"That sounds perfect." Soon enough, she has a backpack filled with sandwiches and chips, and we're on the road. She's in a little sundress, this one short and pink, and I know she isn't wearing any panties.

How do I know? Well, my girl lifted the hem of her dress before we left my apartment to tease me.

I told her it wasn't fair and she just said she wanted

her pussy bare as she rode on the back of my bike. "The vibrations get me all horny, and so wet, Ranger."

I growled in her ear, squeezed her cute ass, and off we rode.

The sun shines down on us and the light breeze is the perfect balm. When we descend Hollow Oak Hill, a valley spreads out before us, and a big lake shines bright at the basin. Ruby squeezes my back. "It's beautiful," she breathes.

"It's Hollow Lake," I tell her. "Crystal clear water."

When we get off the bike, it feels good to stretch our legs, and we've found a secluded spot with a big willow tree overhanging the water. "Is that a rope?" she asks, pointing to a tree branch.

I grin, already pulling off my shirt and kicking off my boots. "Looks like it. Wanna jump in?"

She laughs. "I didn't pack a suit."

I look around, no one in sight. "Have you ever skinny dipped, Miss Ruby?"

She sets her hands on her hips. "What do you think, Ranger?"

I laugh, picking her up off the ground and swinging her around. "I think you're dying to get out of those clothes."

She licks her lips. "I think you're a bad influence on me," she says with a smile as she lifts the hem of her dress.

"That's not what you were screaming last night."

She laughs, loud. And so do I. My girl was coming so hard last night, so loud, that the bed broke. Literally — the headboard came clean off the back.

"Okay, so maybe I have a naughty streak previously undiscovered."

She lets her dress fall to the grass, and I pull my girl into my arms. God, her skin is hot and so damn kissable. But before I can explore every inch of her, she is jumping away, moving over the grass toward the willow tree.

"Careful," I call after her, but she just laughs.

"I may have grown up sheltered, but we were allowed to climb trees." She takes hold of the rope and swings across the clear lake water. The higher she reaches, the faster my heart beats — but then she lets go, dropping into the lake with a crash.

When her head pops up, she's laughing, her eyes as bright as the water, and she is calling at me to get in.

I follow her lead and grab the rope, swinging into the water. It's a shock at first, how cold it is, but then my body gets used to it, relishing the contrast to the beating summer sun.

I swim to her and she wraps her body around mine. My feet touch the ground and I kiss her cheeks, her nose. She's laughing, and so am I. "I don't think I've ever felt so free," I tell her. "You make me feel so alive, Ruby."

He eyelashes flutter, her freckled cheeks washed clean. "It's like I was waiting my whole life for you."

"You have me now," I tell her.

"You think it's real?"

Her question catches me off-guard. "Hell yeah, I do. I love you, Ruby."

It surprises me when she doesn't say it back. I have

no doubt in my mind how I feel about her, for us. But her hesitation says more than I am prepared to handle.

"You don't feel it?" I press.

"I feel it... I just..." She wraps her arms more tightly around me. "I may have grown up in the church, but I don't have much faith in forever. In love."

"Do you have faith in us?"

She swallows. "I feel like the other shoe is gonna drop, Ranger. That I'm gonna wake up and you'll be gone."

I tense, the water growing cold. "When I finished my time with the Army and heard my favorite bar was looking for a manager, I took the position. Joined the Heartlands MC shortly after. Been here a year now and haven't looked back. I'm not going anywhere. The question is, are you?"

She slips from my arms, dipping her head under the water, and when she comes back up for air, I see that her eyes are filled with fear. "I'm scared of this being too good to be true. Of you being too good to be true, Ranger."

I grab her hand before she can swim away again. "I love you, Ruby. Have faith in us."

"I want to," she says, running her hand over my chest. "But I don't even know your real name. I don't know your plans for the future. I don't know anything."

"That's not true," I tell her. "Don't minimize this because you're scared."

She wraps her arms around my neck and I lift her up, her legs wrapping around me too. I carry her from the water and lay her down on the blanket we brought.

I lean over her, memorizing her bare skin, the rise and fall of her breasts, her belly button, her creamy thighs. "Before you came into my life, I hadn't slept a full night in years. I was haunted by things I've seen, things I've done. And then you came along and I could rest. In your arms, Ruby, I found peace. I love you. And you don't need to say it back. But you do need to know it's the goddamn truth."

She swallows, pulling me toward her. "Before you, I didn't think... didn't believe men like you existed." Tears fall from her eyes.

"I'm real, Ruby. And I'm yours."

She doesn't say she loves me, doesn't promise me forever. But she kisses me deeply, hard. She pulls me close, opening her legs and offering me what she is able to give. Maybe not her whole heart, but a piece of it. And I take it with open arms.

I make love to Ruby the way she deserves, the way she craves, the only way I know how — with all of me.

My cock is hard for her, and I ease open her tight little cunt, my fingers opening her sweetness until it's nice and juicy, ready for me. She arches her back, those big tits bouncing, her nipples pointed to the sky. I kiss them, tasting her perfect nipples between my teeth, my cock raging with want as I finger her nice and good, her pussy squeaking with pleasure as I flick her clit, her whimpers turning to full-on moans.

I dip my mouth to her opening, needing to taste the cream of my lover. My beard tickles her and she laughs, pushing my head deeper against her cunt. God, she loves it when I devour her. She better get used to it.

Because this isn't changing. Ever. She is mine now, and soon enough she will feel it the same way I do.

This is real.

"I love you," I tell her, my cock pressing into her. Filling her up until she is gasping.

"Don't stop," she begs, threading her fingers through my hair, kissing my neck, my ears, holding onto me as if for dear life.

I make love to her, the pair of us coming in unison, like it was planned that way all along. And maybe it was.

I hold her in my arms as we finish, searching her eyes for whatever she is holding back. I found her caught in the rain, and that single storm seemed to wash my pain away.

But she's still caught in those clouds. Wrapped up in something I can't quite see.

I hold her tight, knowing whatever it is she's scared of, I'm even more scared of losing her.

10

———

RUBY

AFTER MAKING love under the willow tree, we dress, then fall asleep for hours. With the warmth of the day surrounding us. I wake in Ranger's arms, but he is still sleeping, and so I watch the water, thinking about the words he offered so freely — *I love you.*

Can he really? Is that how true love works?

Wouldn't know the first thing about it... all I know about relationships is what I saw modeled at my father's church. Women who were taught to be quiet, the men who kept them under their thumbs... boys growing up to be men just like their fathers. Daughters growing up to be servants to their men. It may be a modern era for the rest of the world, but for the small slice of earth where my father's church thrives, the community is tight-knit and holds their values close.

Too close.

And my father wanted to build another wing onto the church. Slider was willing to pay for it.

He was a man who ended up at my father's church

after claiming he had found God. He wore the right suits, memorized the right scripture, but I saw the way he looked at me — like he wanted to devour me.

And not in the welcome way Ranger does.

Slider would corner me in hallways, not threatening exactly, but warning me how to behave, telling me what kind of wife he wanted. He'd tell me that when he had me, he would never let me out of his sight.

It made my skin crawl, my throat go dry. Lydia got the same creeped out vibe from him — he always looked a bit too long at us, as if plotting something.

I shake at the memory, and it startles Ranger awake.

"Hey, you okay?" he asks, kissing my cheek.

I tell him about Slider, not wanting to keep secrets from him.

"I couldn't marry a man like that, who saw me as his property. Not his partner. I'm going to go to the city," I explain to Ranger. "And once I get a place set up, I will go back for my sister. She needs a stable home, a safe home."

Ranger cuts in, "You can bring her here."

I hesitate, not wanting empty promises.

His eyes turn dark. "You're really leaving?"

"The plan was always to go to the city and get a place set up for Lydia and me."

Ranger frowns. "So you'll go, just like that?"

"Well..." I bite my bottom lip. "I can't just stay in your apartment. Roxanne said I could work nights at the bar and make some cash—"

"You aren't working in the bar. You can't."

I lift my eyebrows. "What do you mean, I can't?"

"I mean no woman of mine is working there."

I shake my head, incredulous. "Are you seriously telling me what I can and cannot do?"

"You really want to work there?"

"No, I want to make meals and wash clothes and have a simple life, but I don't have a choice. I have to make money, Ranger. I have to get to the city. For Lydia."

"We all have choices," he says coolly.

"Easy for you to say." I stand, shaking out the blanket and packing up the bag.

"So that's it? Conversation over?"

I swallow. "You're just like him. You think I'm someone you can order around."

"No, I'm not, Ruby. I know you. You can't work in the bar because it would make you unhappy—"

"It's good enough for Roxanne."

"But you're not Roxanne. She loves shooting the shit with the bikers. She has different dreams than you."

We stand there, staring at one another. I don't know what he wants and I certainly don't know what to give. I feel stuck, over my head. I thought opening up to him about Slider would help us... instead, we've grounded to a halt, going nowhere.

"I want to go back to the apartment," I tell him. "I want to get back before dark."

He nods, hands me my helmet. "I love you, Ruby, but I don't love you pushing me away."

I don't answer. I don't know *how* to answer. I'm

scared. More scared than I was the day I ran away. This time, I'm scared that the man I'm holding onto as we zoom down the highway is the same as every other man. Out to own me.

When we get back to Ride or Die, I head to the studio and Ranger says he's going to cool down with a beer.

It's been a long day, and the sun has long since set. Knowing we both need a bit of space, I head upstairs and wash my face, trying to get a handle on myself.

I make a cup of tea, and even though it's still warm out, inside I feel cold — chilled to the bone. Like I've made a massive mistake.

And after only a few sips of the chamomile, I know in my gut that I have. It doesn't take me long to realize what I really wanted Ranger to say.

I wanted him to say this... *Stay here with me. Be with me. We will get Lydia and we can make this work. I need you with me.*

Instead, he told me I couldn't be a bartender.

It makes me mad, thinking about what I wanted and what I got.

I need to tell him how I feel, what I really want.

Because what I really want is him. And I need to know if he wants me too.

I leave the apartment, taking the steps two at a time, my heart beating as I berate myself for pushing Ranger away. Choosing to believe the worst instead of the best.

I wave hello to Bulldog at the entrance. "You okay?" he asks.

I nod. "Yeah, just need Ranger." He lets me inside, and I look around the dark bar, trying to find Ranger.

What I see instead stops me in my tracks.

Makes my blood go cold.

Ice cold.

My stomach rolls as I watch the man I've been sleeping with clap my ex-fiancé on the back, clinking beers.

Ranger and Slider and talking like they are old friends. Friends.

I'm in a trance, standing near the exit, covering my mouth as sobs threaten to escape.

Has he been lying his whole time? Ranger and Slider in on some conspiracy together?

When Slider pulls out his phone and snaps a selfie with Ranger, I feel my worst fear confirmed.

"Congratulations, man," Ranger says. "You're getting married tomorrow!" Then he calls Stella over. "We need a bottle of Jameson. I got to take a shot with my buddy."

Slider is still getting married? Does he think I am coming back? Or is there someone else?

My stomach falls. Lydia.

"I live about eight hours away. Long ass trip home, but it'll be worth it when I get there tomorrow. She's a real beauty, my bride," I hear Slider say. "She's not exactly legal, but the laws are nice to men like me here. So long as a parent signs off, you can marry 'em young."

I can't stay any longer. I can't listen to this.

I have to go. Now.

I leave the bar with tears streaming down my face and practically fall into Roxanne's arms.

"Sweetie? What is it?"

I shake my head. Not wanting to put words to this.

"What do you need, Ruby? What's happening?"

"I have to go home." My voice shakes. "My sister... I need to see my sister..."

"Okay, want me to get Ranger?" she asks, searching my eyes. But I can't meet her gaze. I'm too devastated.

I grab Roxanne's hand. "No. I don't want him to know. Swear you won't tell him?"

She follows me up the stairs to the apartment. I start shoving clothes in a tote bag, not really caring what stays behind. Only caring about seeing Lydia. Getting her away from my father's house before Slider gets his claws in her.

I know he was talking about marrying her. I was sure she would be safe, given how young she is. But it turns out, he's even more of a sick bastard than I thought he was. She is too young. So innocent. It's not fair.

"You're scaring me, Ruby."

"I just need some money for a cab. I will pay you back, I promise. Actually, here," I say, sliding my mother's diamond ring from my right ring finger. It was her engagement ring and I found it in my father's things before I ran away. "Pawn this."

"I'm not pawning that," she says. Reaching into her purse, she hands me a wad of cash wrapped with a rubber band. "It's five hundred dollars. But you better swear to me you'll call me in a few hours to let me know you're okay." She jots down her number and presses it into my palm. "And maybe use that cash to buy a phone."

"I'll pay you back," I say, taking the stairs two at a time while Stella follows. I rush over to one of the many cabs in the parking lot and open the back door. "And please don't tell Ranger."

"I promise I won't tell Ridge. So long as you promise to call."

"Ridge?" I ask, swallowing as I slide into the back seat.

"Yeah. His real name's Ridge."

I nod, feeling like this simple fact is a punch to the gut. What did I really know about Ranger? I didn't know his real name, or apparently his friends. I knew nothing except what I wanted to see.

"Right, of course," I say, then I wave goodbye, pulling the door shut.

I tell the cab driver the address to my father's house, knowing it's the nail in my coffin.

But hopefully it will save my sister's life.

I PUSH BACK from the bar stool, bottle of whiskey in hand. "What did you say?" I ask Joe, an old buddy from the Army I haven't seen in a few years. Last time I saw him, he was going through a hell of a time, in trouble with his commanding officer or something — but I never got the full story. I avoided gossip all my life, and when I was a Ranger, it wasn't any different.

"Shit, man, it's all good. She's a good girl."

"What the fuck are you talking about? Marrying a child?"

Joe laughs, a grin on his face that looks a bit more sinister than I like. "She might not like the arrangement, but her virgin cunt is gonna like my co—" He grabs his junk just as I pull him off his stool and push him against the wall.

The bar breaks out in roars as everybody looks on. I have him against the wall and am not backing down. "You're forcing her to marry you against her will?"

He struggles against me, but I've got my hands tight

around his shirt collar, smashing him against the wall. "Her father agreed to it. And she knows better than to make him mad — not after her older sister already pissed him off. Was supposed to be marrying her tomorrow, but plans changed." He laughs. "Lucky me."

"Sister?" The blood drains from my face. This story sounds too similar to another I've been hearing about recently. Ruby's story. My blood runs cold as I think about the nickname Ruby mentioned. Slider. Joe never went by a nickname in the Army, but with the last name Slidinsky, Slider could definitely be his nickname.

"Slider. You're Joe fucking Slidinsky." Heat rises within me and I want to kill this man here and now. He hurt the woman I love, scarred her and scared her, and I won't let him think he can do it again.

"Stop, I can't breathe," he says, kicking at me. "Help," he says, looking around wildly.

My boys are here now. Killian and Chain and Gage. They pull me off Slider, which is a good fucking thing because I'm out of control. I'm willing — wanting — to kill this man and it seems everyone in the bar knows it.

"You will not get your claws in Lydia, you understand?" I growl at him as Killian and Gage hold him.

"You know Lydia? How?"

I want to punch, wanna fight — but I know that won't help anyone.

"Don't say her name, you piece of shit."

He laughs like the cocky fool he is. "Fuck you," he spits. "You're just jealous I'm getting her tight pussy."

I can't take it anymore, I pull back, swinging at him

with eyes wide open, slamming my fist against his jaw. The crack reverberates throughout the bar and I swear every eye is on me. I don't give a shit. This is my bar, my home. He will not come here and desecrate it. Not on my watch.

"That's enough, Ranger," Killian says. "We'll get him out of here."

I don't care what they do with him, so long as I have Ruby in my arms, so long as I ride with my boys until we get Lydia safe, here, out of harm's way.

"I gotta see Ruby, make sure she's okay." My heart pounds as I take my stairs two at a time, needing to find my girl, pull her into my arms, tell her I hate fighting. Tell her what I really need is her here, with me, always. I got freaked out when she mentioned going to the city. I got scared. Because the idea of her ever leaving me, ever being in this big, wild world without me by her side, scares the shit out of me.

Not because I don't think she can handle herself, but because there are plenty of men like Slider — wolves in sheep's clothing — and I don't want her to get hurt. Couldn't bear it.

"Ruby," I call, opening my apartment door... but there is no one here. *She's not here.* My pulse quickens as I look around, hoping I'm wrong, that she's here, in the bathroom, under the blankets... but no. She isn't anywhere. My apartment is empty.

No. This can't be happening. I run downstairs, see my bouncer. "Where's Slider, that fucker I just punched?"

"Shit, man, he was here with some buddies. Fhey found him all beat up and they just left."

Fuck. I punch a wall, my fist burning, but the anger rises up inside me so damn fast. "Have you seen Ruby? Anywhere?"

He looks around. "She was with Roxanne earlier. Want me to get her? She's not working tonight but I think she's in the garage with Maddox."

I nod and he runs off.

When she comes to me, her eyes are filled with worry. "Oh shit, what happened?"

I explain the Slider situation, asking if she knows where Ruby's at.

"She made me promise not to tell."

"Listen to me," I say, my eyes filling with goddamn tears. "I can't lose her. I love her. You understand? And now she's in trouble." I explain about her sister, the wedding, and Roxy shakes her head, shocked.

"Oh God." Roxanne covers her mouth, tears brimming in her eyes. "I was trying to do the right thing. She didn't want you to know... She was upset, but I wasn't going to question her."

"Just tell me what happened," I say, trying my goddamn best to keep my cool.

"She mentioned her sister. Said she had to go help her. Had to go get her. I gave her five hundred bucks and made her promise to call me once she got somewhere safe."

"You what?" I drag my hands through my hair, trying to steady my breath.

"It's her right to do what she wants, Ranger, but I would never have let her go if I'd known."

"Fuck." I slam my fist into my open palm. "Any idea where she's headed?"

Roxanne shakes her head. "I'm so sorry."

I just know what road I found her on, but I never asked what her father's church is called, what town it's in... I got the impression it's off the grid with a low profile. Slider said he lives about eight hours away, which could mean a hell of a lot of places. And considering the first exit after the bar is a four-way interstate — he could be going any direction within ten minutes.

"Fuck!" I growl. "Is there a card on file for Slider? Any chance I can get an address?"

Roxanne nods. "I'll go find out. Use your computer and see if you can find him online."

I nod, telling her to let the club know what's up. We have to find Ruby, come hell or high water.

She is my life, my love. And I can't lose her. Not now, not like this.

12

RUBY

By the time I get off the Greyhound bus, my body aches. I cried for hours on the bus before I fell asleep, but it was hard. I kept waking up, my head leaning against the window, praying that everything that happened last night was a dream. A terrible nightmare.

But when the bus makes its final stop and I step off the platform back in Dixieville, I'm wide awake.

I know what I must do.

Getting in yet another taxi, I give my father's address, headed to the house where I will await my future.

It's early dawn. The sky is just beginning to rise and it's just five a.m. I tell the taxi driver to drop me off half a mile from home. I walk quickly down the dusty road to my father's house and climb on top of an old lawn chair so I can access the window to the bedroom Lydia and I shared. It's already half open — the old house doesn't have central air so we keep the windows open and fans going day and night in the summer months.

I climb through the window into the most familiar room of my life. Pale pink walls, worn wood floors, a yellow wool rug between our beds. The rug we knelt on each night as we said our prayers. Bowing our heads and hoping for a sign. Salvation. A way out of the life we had.

Tears fill my eyes as I see my sweet sister sound asleep. The bedroom door is closed, and I know my father won't be up for a few hours.

We have time.

I kneel before her bed, taking her hand in mine, sweeping her hair from her face. My sister who I raised, who is my best friend and only confidante.

"Lydia," I whisper. "Hey, I'm home."

Her eyes blink open sleepily, confused at first, and then she shakes her head, tears spilling onto her cheeks as she sits up. "Ruby?"

I press a finger to my lips.

She nods in understanding. Soft blonde hair falling in her face, morning light streaking through the window, she seems to glow. "What are you doing here?" she whispers, scooting over in the bed and letting me crawl in beside her.

I explain as quickly as possible what happened... how the car caught on fire, how Ranger saved me... how I gave myself to him.

"You did?" Lydia gasps, covering her mouth. "You love him?"

I sigh, pressing my hand to hers. "Oh sweetie, I thought I did."

"What happened? Why are you here?"

I explain seeing Slider in the bar, how Ranger and he were clearly friends. And how I heard Slider say he was getting married. Today.

"Is it true?" I ask. "Are you being forced to take my place?"

Lydia's chin trembles, her shoulders shake, and I pull her close, letting her cry. "As soon as Father realized you'd left, truly left, Slider was angry. Right away, Father offered him me — without even a blink. Slider's been in Jonesboro on business with his men. I know whatever they do is shady, but Father won't hear of it. Slider is set to arrive this morning, right before the wedding."

"I won't let that happen," I tell her.

"There is no stopping it, especially if Ranger isn't what you hoped he was... you can't go back there."

"No, but you can go. I will stay and marry Slider, and you can take a bus to Jonesboro. I have money."

"I'm not leaving you." She cries against my shoulder. Holding me tight. "We have to stick together."

"Then we both go, right now. We can run and we can get away, Lydia."

Lydia hesitates, and I see a familiar fear in her eyes. Finally, she nods. "Okay," she says. "Let's go. I don't want to be alone anymore."

Silently, we pack a bag for her, and she dresses quickly. Her cat, Muffins, is on her bed and she leans down to give her a big kiss, crying as she does.

We hear our father upstairs, getting out of bed. Heavy footsteps. My pulse quickens. I won't be caught in his web again. We have to hurry.

Wordlessly, we climb out the window, knowing the bus stop is just five miles away. We can run there, through the woods, and not be seen.

We tiptoe over the gravel driveway, our feet crunching as we move quickly toward the back meadow that is covered in clover. But as we go, Slider's big black pick-up truck rolls up, and he honks his horn hard when he sees us.

"Where you going?" he hollers, jumping out of the truck, his buddies Lionel and Jordy jumping out of the cab. "Get back here," he shouts.

We crouch low, scared. "We can't get away," I say, clutching Lydia's hands. Wishing we'd left a few minutes earlier.

"Just don't leave me," she says and my heart breaks. Days ago when I drove away, I thought leaving was the right thing to do... but now that I see how hard this must have been on her, I know I should have taken her with me, our father be damned.

Tears fill my eyes. Did I leave Ranger in the exact same way? Without asking him to explain? To help me understand? No... he is friends with Slider — that alone tells me everything I need to know.

Doesn't it?

It doesn't matter now. Because now Slider and my father are running toward Lydia and me, reaching us with arms outstretched, a gun in Slider's hand. There isn't a chance in hell they will let us go.

"What do you think you're doing?" my father shouts, his hand on my arm, tugging me to stand.

"Didn't want to miss the wedding, did you?" Slider

says. I take a look at him. His eye is black, his jaw is bloody. Someone roughed him up really good. "We were set to marry in a few hours. But considering you're a runner, we might as well head out now. The original plan is back on, I take it, Leroy?"

Father nods. "Looks like Ruby came home just in time."

His words make little sense, and Lydia is hysterical. "Why, Father? Why are you doing this?" she cries. "We don't need a bigger church. We just—"

Slider cackles and my Father sneers. "Your girls still think this is about the church?" he asks. Slider looks down at us. "Your father happens to have two virgin brides I can sell for a pretty penny down in Mexico. Though, when I convinced him to give me Lydia, I realized I wanted her for myself. Lucky me."

Horror snakes through me. "What is he saying?"

Father must know he's lost our respect — not that he has ever had it. "He'll give me plenty for each of you. I can't pass that up. Not when there are so many good folks here in Dixieville who could use the leg up."

Slider laughs. Looking at my father like he is a fool. "Let's not forget the thousands you owe me."

My father's eyes fall to the ground, and my stomach turns. My father isn't a man of God... he has been doing things under the cover of the church... things I don't want to think about.

"Let's go, then," he says. Lionel and Jordy have duct tape and burlap sacks in hand. "Give them the sleeping pills and we can get to the airport. Soon enough, we will be on a private jet headed to Punta Cana."

Lydia and I lock eyes. If their plan works, we might be flying across international waters within a few hours. Never to be seen again.

I can't go.

I close my eyes, terrified of being separated from my sister, terrified of being sold as a sex slave, terrified of never seeing Ranger again.

I'm tossed over Jordy's shoulder and the other man lifts Lydia from the ground. They carry us toward the farmhouse. We're both kicking and screaming. Scared. Tears fall down my face as they carelessly cross the field. The morning sun is just rising and I wish I could go back to sleep, pretend this wasn't happening. But I can't rewrite history — I can only move forward, praying that this isn't how my story ends.

And then, it starts pouring. Rain ripping through the sky, thunder clapping, lightning striking, and through it all is a wild, reckless noise.

I look up, and coming toward us is the Heartlands MC. Riding as one, a brotherhood. A family. The cavalry riding in tight formation, the heavy throb of their engines coming over the hill.

Tears flood my eyes and my heart holds out hope. Ranger came for me. For us.

Lydia and I are not going down without a fight.

13

It took hours to figure out where Ruby's father lived. Finally, we figured it out from one photo Joe Slidinsky posted on Facebook. A Google search later, a fee paid to access a record of Ruby's birth certificate, and we knew exactly where her father lived. In Dixieville.

Took us seven hours to ride here, all through the night. The whole time I rode, my heart pounded as fear gripped my chest. Not wanting the worst to be true.

I try not to be pissed at anyone besides myself that Slider got away. I'd have killed him if he'd stuck around and I don't want blood on my hands, even if I do want him to pay.

When the white farmhouse comes into view, Heartlands MC rallies. The men come together in formation as we ride toward the woman I love.

I saw love happen before my very eyes. Because it happened to me. I know what is possible. And I know love like that is worth the fight. Ruby is worth fighting for, even if she doesn't think so.

And now, as we ride up to the farmhouse, I know trouble is afoot. There is shouting in the distance. I see two women slung over the shoulders of two men, and there's at least one gun raised.

Signaling with my hands, I tell Killian to call the local cops. We ride closer, but with caution. We came here for the girls, not for a goddamn bloodbath.

The men on the porch turn to us as we get off our bikes. We approach them with righteous anger brewing in our hearts.

There she is.

Ruby.

Right there.

And Slider has a gun pointed straight at me.

"Who the hell is this?" a man shouts. I'm guessing it's Ruby's dad.

"Are you fucking with me?" Slider shouts my way as the men I rode with stand beside me.

"They aren't your property, Slider," I shout. "Let the women go."

"Or what?"

I reach behind my back, ready to draw, but hold off. Ruby is too close to start shooting. "I'm not fucking around. This ends now."

"You never liked killing. No way are you going to kill an old Army buddy," Slider hisses.

"You were in the Army together?" Ruby asks, still in the arms of a strange man.

I walk closer, not scared of these fuckers. "Yes. That is how I know Joe Slidinsky. Apparently, he goes as

Slider now. Hadn't seen him in years... and damn, has he changed."

"But I thought... I..." Her eyes fill with tears, but there is no time for a reunion. Not when Slider's guys are looking for a fight. Heartlands joins me and together, we push off the threat. Killian pushes a man against the front door, trying to get him away from the younger girl. Chain charges at the other man, who holds Ruby hostage.

But Slider doesn't like us messing with his plan. Slider's gun is tucked in his belt, and I rush him, hoping to knock him off his feet so whatever he is planning on shooting is off target.

Before I can, he pulls the trigger, a bullet flying, finding its way to my chest.

It happens so damn fast. One minute I have my eyes on the prize, the next minute I am falling on the ground, blood seeping from the bullet hole, my life flashing before my eyes.

"No!" Ruby screams, her terror reverberating through us all, hitting me square in the heart. She falls to the ground at my side as Killian uses the opportunity to grab Slider from behind, pushing him off the porch and onto the ground.

Sirens blare from a distance. Ruby leans over me, her father bellowing like the mad man he is. Her fingers tracing my face.

"I can't lose you," she cries. "Not when I just realized I love you."

"You love me, baby?" I ask, my voice shaky. My vision is fading. It's dark out here, in the wide wilderness of the great unknown. Damn, I didn't want to die so soon.

"I love you, Ridge," she says, kissing me. "I love you so much."

And then my eyes close.

And they don't open up again.

———

THE ROOM IS bright white and smells like cleaning supplies. I jerk up, trying to remember what got me here — riding all night, a fight, a bullet. *I love you.*

"Ranger?" Ruby's sweet voice pulls me back to the land of the living. "Thank God, you're awake. Oh, I thought I lost you."

"I'm right here, baby," I say, my mouth tasting like cotton, my body aching head to toe. A nurse comes in, followed by a doctor. They check my vitals, discuss my condition, but I can't concentrate on them. I only have eyes for her. Ruby. The love of my fucking life.

"You love me, huh?" I look her over. She looks like she's been crying for hours. I hate that I might have caused some of those tears.

"So much," she says, wiping her eyes. "I shouldn't have left. I thought you and Slider were in on something... I thought the worst when I should have assumed the best. Forgive me, Ranger. Please."

"I'll take a bullet for you any day."

"Don't say that," she says tearfully. "I've been so scared. I thought I lost you."

"I'm not going anywhere."

The doctor coughs. "Sorry to interrupt this reunion, but I wanted to update you, Ridge."

I nod. "Give it to me straight."

"You were in surgery for three hours. The bullet entered the right side of your chest. You had broken ribs and a punctured lung. And had it been a few inches to the left, well, that would have been the end of it. But thankfully, here you are. Surgery was a success and it looks like your intervention just helped the state round up the criminals they have been after for the last year. The cops are waiting to have a word with you when you're up for it."

I look to Ruby. She nods. "Slider and his crew have been operating a drug ring and a sex trafficking operation. More than one girl's life has been saved."

The doctor shakes my hand and tells me he'll be back in a few hours. The nurse leaves after finishing my vitals and giving me some pain medication in my IV.

"Slider always seemed a little off in the Army, but I gave him the benefit of the doubt, knowing the situation was stressful." I shake my head. "Damn, I hate that you thought he and I... Ruby, you gotta know I'm not that sort of man."

She sits on the edge of my hospital bed. "I know that now. I was already in a bad place, uncertain of what you wanted... what we were... and I knew I needed to get Lydia... so I pulled back emotionally. When I saw you with him, it felt like the confirmation of my worst fears."

"I told you I love you. You must know what I want."

She shakes her head. "Ranger, I'm not like you. I

don't have the same faith that you have. I've been living in a state of fear. So, the idea that someone — you — are willing to stick up for me, choose me... truly love me... it is hard to believe."

Her words make sense, even if they are difficult to process. We've both been through hell — her entire life, and my time in the military. I wish none of this had happened — but I hope that now she knows the truth. The MC isn't a bunch of bad guys — we're the ones willing to fight for the people we love. And so am I.

"Do you believe it now? Believe in us?"

She nods, running her hand gently over the bandages on my chest. "I do, Ranger," she whispers, tears falling down her porcelain cheeks. "I thought I lost you, my one true thing. But here we are, a second chance... and I won't waste it."

I clear my throat, not wanting to waste one minute more. "So you'll marry me?"

She laughs lightly. "I think the nurse gave you too high a dose of those meds."

I shake my head, taking her hand. "I know exactly what I'm asking. Be my wife. My partner. My everything. Marry me, Ruby."

Tears splash down her cheeks, her face that of an angel. And when she leans over and kisses me, my heart heals.

"I will marry you, Ridge. I will be your wife. But..."

My heart stops, which isn't a good thing when I'm lying in a hospital bed after being shot to within an inch of my life. "But what?"

"But my sister, Lydia... she needs me. My father will

likely face prison time, and she is still a minor. I am responsible for her."

"Of course, you are. We'll get a house big enough for all of us. Don't worry. She is family now. *We* are family now."

"Thank you, Ranger. Thank you so much." She kisses me again, and I feel the weight lifted off her shoulders.

"So what do you think, a wedding as soon as we get out of here?"

"Why the hurry?" she says with a laugh.

"Life is fucking precious, Ruby."

She nods, her eyes on my bullet wound. "You're right. No time like the present."

I smile. "God, how did a hard ass like me end up with a sweet thing like you?"

She bites her bottom lip. "Oh Ranger, you must be delirious." She slides her hand under my bedsheets, running her fingers over my thick cock. "I'm not as sweet as some might think."

I groan, wishing like hell I wasn't so banged up. But thanking my lucky stars it's Ruby who is here, nursing me back to health.

14

RUBY

Six weeks later...

THE SUN SHINES BRIGHTLY, and I look to my sister, Lydia, who is beside herself with happiness. "Do I look okay?" I ask, smoothing the bodice of my gown.

She is kneeling and fluffing the skirt of my wedding dress, and she beams up at me. "You look like a Bohemian princess."

I laugh, looking at myself in the floor length mirror in Ranger's apartment. I am wearing a flower crown of pale pink roses and Queen Anne's lace, and a vintage dress that has a long lace train. This is a wedding day I never dreamed of for myself, and yet, it's here. I keep pinching myself to make sure this isn't all a dream.

"I can't believe this is really happening," I say, my heart so full.

"I can. Gosh, the way Ranger looks at you..." Lydia shakes her head, her long hair in waves down her back.

"It's so romantic." She stands and smooths out her own soft pink, knee length dress.

"You sure you'll be okay here without me?" I ask. "It will only be three days but if you need me back sooner, just call."

Lydia hands me my bouquet of wildflowers. "Stop, I'll be fine. Do you see how overprotective all these bikers are? Besides, Roxanne is staying here at the apartment with me, and she isn't going to let anything happen."

"That's true, she's like a mama bear. The fiercest and most protective twenty-three-year-old I've ever met." After I left to return to my father's farm, Roxanne felt terrible for letting me go after she realized what I was walking into. But she wasn't to blame for any of it. I chose to go on my own and it was certainly not her fault. That was all on me.

But now she is extra cautious of Lydia, which makes me feel a heck of a lot better while going on my honeymoon.

"You ladies ready?" Bulldog, the bouncer, sticks his head into the apartment. "The show's about to start."

I smile, feeling peace blossom in my heart. Never having been so happy in my entire life.

"I'm ready," I tell him, and Lydia and I follow him out of the apartment, past the bar, through the parking lot, into the meadow behind the garage. There are nearly a hundred bikes on their kickstands, and my eyes widen in surprise. "Wow, so many people are here."

"The brotherhood sticks together," Bulldog says.

"You'll always be safe now, so long as you let the men of the Heartlands protect you."

Tears fill my eyes and Lydia squeezes my hand. She understands, just like I do, how much that promise means. After a lifetime of being treated so poorly by our own father, the idea of men who stick up for what is right is a true treasure. Slider was locked away, but our father wasn't charged. Still, Lydia and I made a vow to never speak to him again. We're safe now because we have the Heartlands on our side.

"It's go time," Bulldog says as we round the corner to the field where the ceremony is taking place. There are white chairs lined up in rows and a white aisle runner leading the way. An archway at the front is covered in flowers and greenery and there is a bluegrass band playing songs.

There's not a rain cloud in sight.

Lydia walks down the aisle toward the biker marrying us, and standing up there, front and center, is Ranger, my Ridge. The love of my life.

Tears fill my eyes as the wedding march begins, everyone standing and turning to face me. It's the wedding of my dreams, my fantasies, and here it is, my real life.

I didn't have faith in real love, but Ranger changed all that. He changed me.

I walk toward him with eyes as bright as the blue, cloudless sky. I walk toward him with a heart full of promise. I walk toward him knowing I will keep walking toward this man for the rest of my life.

He is my heart, my soul, my whole wide world. And I'm lucky enough to be his wife.

———

WE CHECK into the hotel on Hollow Lake eagerly. I've been on the back of my husband's bike for the last few hours and I'm so ready to have something besides a vibrating hog between my legs. I want him.

So badly.

He slides the key into the lock and opens the door for us, then he picks me up, and carries me over the threshold. I laugh as he gallantly kicks the door shut, leaving us alone for the first time as husband and wife.

He lowers my feet to the ground, kissing me as he does. I'm in a white tank top and white jeans — having changed after out reception at Ride or Die. The bar is probably in full-on party mode by now, but we left at dusk, wanting to ride off into the sunset.

Now, here we are, husband and wife.

"Today was perfect," I tell him as my feet touch the ground. "And I want tonight to be perfect too."

"It will be," he tells me, his voice low and gruff. Intense. His eyes lock on mine and his hands cup my cheeks. "God, I love you, Ruby. I am so damn proud to be your man."

"Don't make me cry," I whisper, the moment hushed and sacred. Ours.

"I won't let you down. I mean it. I vow to be the man you need."

A tear falls from my eyes and Ranger brushes it

with his calloused thumb. "I know what I need from you now," I tell him with bated breath. "I need you against me."

He runs his hands over my back, lifting my tank top off, and I shimmy out of my jeans. I stand before him in a white lace bra and a thong that barely covers my freshly waxed pussy.

"God, you are gorgeous," he growls in my ear, pulling me close. "Your tits look fucking perfect in this."

I smile, reaching for his belt. He helps me out, undressing quickly. I shake my head. "The boxers too."

He grins, lifting his eyebrows. "Bossy."

I smile. "Happy wife, happy life."

He steps toward me, his thick cock at attention. "That better?"

I drop to my knees and run my fingers over his thick shaft. "I love how big you are, Ranger. How you feel in my mouth."

I open wide for him, taking his still rod in my parted lips, sucking off the man who makes my pussy drip with pleasure. I want to make him drip with pleasure too. Want him to come in my mouth and I want to swallow every last drop of his seed. As one of my first acts as his wife, I want to get him off on my knees. Begging for more.

"Oh God," he groans as I suck him the way he likes. Slowly, bopping my head up and down as his cock hits my throat, I run my fingers over his balls. They are tight and hot, and I move my mouth over them, sucking them one at a time. His hard, veiny cock is dripping with precome and I lick it off with my tongue, swirling his pink tip in my mouth, savoring the drop.

I want more. We move to the bed and I straddle him backward, and I dip my head again, sucking him with my ass in Ranger's face.

"Oh, oh, ohhhh," I moan loudly as he pulls down my thong, spreading my ass cheeks, pressing his mouth to my wet hole, his beard tickling me and his fingers dipping into my pussy, the place he knows I love.

He begins fingering me nice and good, licking me too, making me squirm atop him, making it hard to concentrate on his thick cock, but I do my best, licking him as he sucks me, our fluid motion one of love, of devotion, and my cunt begs for release as he adds a second, then a third finger to my center.

"Oh fuck, baby, you're coming so hard." He squeezes my ass, his mouth buried in my pussy, and I suck harder, with a deep longing for his come to slide down my throat and warm my core.

I'm so wet, though, and he knows I need a different sort of attention. He rolls me onto my back, spreading my knees nice and wide, and then he begins to massage my clit nice and slow. I reach for his cock, but I can't touch it. He pins me down, his hungry eyes the only thing I see — my focus, and my desire.

He gets me off, eyes locked with mine. Fingering me until I am panting, moaning, my come squirting against him. My eyes widen, having never down that before, quite like that.

He grins, pulling my breast into his mouth, sucking

my nipple, his palm rubbing against my cunt. My whole body is shaking as an orgasm runs through me.

"Oh, Ranger," I moan, my body his. When I finish, I get that desperate need inside of me. He straddles me, coming closer, placing his big, thick cock between my breasts, and massaging himself between them.

I want his come all over me, coating my breasts, my neck, my face. He pumps himself against me and I lick my lips with need. "Come all over," I whimper as his cock erupts on my skin, coating me the way I dreamt. He pumps his big shaft, the ribbons of come on my breasts, and I open my mouth, wanting to catch some of his creamy release. He helps me, placing his big cock in my mouth, letting me swallow as he finishes, my belly warm with him and my body made for him, and my core still hot for him.

"Come in me again," I beg, and he listens. His cock grows hard, my fingers stroking him, my body slick with his release, his body slick with mine. We are wrapped up in one another in the most glorious way.

"I love you, Ruby," he whispers in my ear as his cock moves inside my willing pussy. "I love you so goddamn much."

"I love you too, Ranger."

We move together in a rhythm all our own, our moaning turning to cries as we get off, for the first time, as husband and wife.

EPILOGUE 1

RANGER

One year later….

She was a beautiful bride, but this is next-level sexy.

Ruby is big and round, carrying the twins, and she somehow makes it seem effortless. I've heard more than one woman complain about it, but whenever someone stops Ruby at the grocery store and asks how she is feeling, she always tells them it's amazing, her face glowing with pride.

She was made to do this.

God, I feel like the luckiest man in the world.

"It looks so good," Lydia says as Ruby and I show off the new addition we made just for her. We bought a house a quarter-mile from the bar and garage, but it needed a bit of extra room. Lydia has been sleeping in what will be the nursery, but getting this space set up for her before the babies arrived was our priority. "Thank you. You've done so much for me."

"You're my little sister — I'd move mountains for

you," Ruby says.

"I know, but still." She blinks back tears, a crier like her sister. "You know what I mean, Ruby. It is just so much goodness after so much struggle."

"I know," Ruby says, giving her sister an awkward hug. Her eight-months-pregnant belly makes everything a little more difficult. Well, not *everything*. Some things just require more creativity. "What are you smiling about, Ranger?"

I grin, knowing my thoughts about pulling Ruby onto our bed aren't exactly appropriate to mention out loud. "I'm just thinking how lucky we are."

Lydia groans, laughing. She always gives me a hard time about being too damn sentimental. And I suppose I am. But she has become like a daughter to me, strange as that might sound. I am her legal guardian now, and I won't let anything happen to her. And I also want her to know she is not going to be forgotten just because the twins are on their way. That is why Ruby and I made sure the addition was finished in time.

"And you have a private entrance, and a private bathroom," Ruby says, showing it all off. "And that lavender bedding we got last week will go so great with the wall color, don't you think?"

Lydia smiles, running her hand over the oak desk in the corner. "I even have a spot for my schoolwork." She lifts her eyebrows. "Unless you've changed your mind and I can do online school for the rest of high school?"

Ruby shakes her head. "No way. You need to have some normal teenage experiences."

Lydia rolls her eyes but there is a teasing smile on

her face. She's just turned seventeen and has a year left before she graduates. School is going to start in a few weeks. "Okay, fine, but do you care if I go on a ride with Jackal?"

Ruby's eyes go wide and she swats at her sister. "He is six years older than you. And a biker!"

I grab her by the waist. "I'm seven years older than you and a biker."

Ruby twists out of my grip, laughing. "Yes, but I was twenty-one when we met. Big difference." Then, turning to her little sister, she adds, "Go find a nice boy in town who is your age."

Lydia laughs, then gives us both hugs. "I have to go work my shift at the ice cream shop. See you tonight, okay?"

After she leaves, Ruby and I go to the kitchen for something to eat but Ruby says she needs to lie down and rest. I follow her into the bedroom and help her take off her shoes, her feet swollen, and rub them for her as she lies on her back.

"Come here," she says softly. "I need you closer."

I move behind her, spooning her on the bed, kissing her neck and resting my arm over her belly. Feeling our babies move. "I can't wait to meet them," I tell her.

"We still need to decide on names."

"I like Harley for the girl," I say. "Even if it is a little on the nose."

"I do too." She takes my hand and kisses my knuckles. "How about R.J. for the boy? Ridge Junior?"

"Really?" I ask, as she turns to face me.

She nods. "I think it would be sweet to name him

after his daddy."

I kiss her, loving her sentimentality, the fact that she seems to understand how much it means.

"I love you, Ruby."

"Same," she says with a sweet smile on her lips. Then she reaches down and runs her hand over my length. "I need you though, so badly."

"Damn woman, this pregnancy has made you insanely horny."

She laughs. "Come on, you know I can't get enough of you either way."

I chuckle, lifting her shirt, exposing her belly and her breasts. I unhook her bra from behind and she pushes down her leggings. I help, then once she is naked, I gently massage her big, full titties, kissing and sucking them. God, she is so sexy, so knocked up and so ready to be a mother. It gets me hard as solid rock. I pull down my pants, and my cock is raging with want. On her back, I open Ruby's knees, needing access to her sweet, ripe cunt.

"Oh, that feels so good," she whimpers as I finger her gently, sweeping my hand over her, rubbing her in circles the way she loves. Then she rolls over onto her hands and knees. "Take me this way, please."

I won't make my woman beg now or ever. I rub her round ass, slipping my hand between her legs to her wet folds. God, she is ready. "I'm so fucking hot for you," I tell her, my cock thick and ready for her pussy.

I fill her up, holding onto her hips as she takes every inch of me. She moans as I plunge deep inside her, thrusting my cock where it belongs. I'm glad the house is empty because my Ruby is loud when she gets off, crying my name, asking for more, more, harder.

I give her what she wants. I fuck her nice and good, her big tits swaying as I give her what she needs, my cock thick and ready to explode. She's gripping the sheets with her hands, dripping as we both get off. "Oh, I'm so close, I'm so... soo... oh, yes. Yes!"

She gets off the way I knew she would, and my cock lets go of all inhibition, my seed sinking deep inside her, my balls smacking her tight cunt as I pound her ripe and ready pussy.

But as soon as she gets up from the bed, she explains. "Oh God, Ranger, I think... I think...."

She looks down. It's obvious her water has broken — it splashes down to her feet, and she covers her mouth. "It's time!"

———

Eight hours later, my beautiful wife is glowing in a whole new way. I'm sitting beside her in a rocking chair, and nestled in my arms are our twins, born four weeks early but healthy as can be. Ruby ended up having an emergency C-section after the babies proved they were happy with where they were. Once Harley's heart rate dropped, however, the doctor and nurses changed course, and they helped us deliver two beautiful babies.

Ruby looks like the angel I always knew her to be. She smiles now, watching as I kiss the heads of her little ones and I keep getting choked up, feeling the monumental responsibility for my family.

Killian and Lydia enter the hospital room, and my buddy claps me on the back. "Saw your minivan in the parking lot."

Chuckling, I punch him in the arm. "Don't make fun of me. It's the top safety rated minivan in the country."

Killian just grins, and I suppose I will be getting a hard time from him for a while. I didn't trade in my bike — hell no, that was my first baby. But I have the keys to a vehicle that can transport my entire family where it needs to go.

Lydia is exclaiming over the babies, and she gently takes R.J. in her arms. "He is so adorable. And he looks just like you, Ranger."

I look over at Ruby, thanking my lucky stars she got out of surgery okay. She smiles at her sister. "Don't get any ideas, Lydia. No baby fever for you."

Lydia laughs. "Don't worry. I don't plan on ever having kids."

"Really?" Killian asks.

"Really. I have big plans."

"What do those include?" Ruby asks, reaching for her cup of water. I help her with it, knowing she is going to have a long few weeks of recovery. I bend the straw for her.

Lydia beams down at her nephew. "I have plans to be the best auntie in the whole wide world!"

Ruby and I lock eyes, the love we feel for our family so big, so wide, stretching out across the room, and further still. Our love reaches across the land of the free and home of the brave.

EPILOGUE 2

RUBY

Five Years later….

When Ranger suggested it, I thought he was joking. "No, I mean it. Let's go on a road trip for our five-year anniversary."

"I was thinking somewhere tropical," I say with a teasing smile. I'm totally joking, but he doesn't need to know that. I have a fear of flying and would much rather spend a week on the back of his bike, clinging to my sweaty and sexy man. Sure, a few days lying on a beach somewhere sounds romantic, but I'd much rather have the bike's vibration between my legs for hours at a time, getting me all revved up for the night ahead.

"Really? A beach or something?"

"Mmhhhmm," I say as I finish packing the twins' lunch boxes for their summer day camp.

"Well, good. I was thinking the same thing."

That gets my attention. "What do you mean? I don't want to fly anywhere."

He chuckles. "I know that. You think you are so funny, but I have news for you. We are taking a road trip, on my bike, but we're headed to the beach. To the coast."

"Really?" My moth falls open. "That sounds... amazing."

"Best of both worlds, baby." He comes up behind me, kissing me on the neck. "Sound good?"

I spin to face him, leaning on the kitchen counter. "You think we can really leave the twins for a week?"

He brushes my hair from my face. "Lydia already agreed to babysit. We leave on Saturday."

I laugh. "But it's Thursday!"

"Perfect — you'll have time to go shopping for a new swimsuit."

I twist my lips, thinking I'll need to get to a salon, too, for a bikini wax. We haven't left the kids for a week before, but we have been talking about having another baby... and maybe a week away would help us with that.

"Sounds perfect," I admit. "I'll download some books on my Kindle, and I'd like some new make up too. Oh, and some..." I stop talking, figuring some things are best left for later.

"What?" Ranger asks, leaning closer. I feel his thick cock against my belly.

"Nothing. I was just thinking if I have time when I'm out, maybe I'll pick up some new lingerie."

He grins. "We only have two saddle bags. You realize that, right?" He kisses me. "How about you do your shopping and I'll get the kids to summer camp. I'll start the grocery shopping and make some lists for Lydia, too."

"You're so good to me," I say, savoring his words.

"And in a day and a half, you can be good to me," he says, taking my hand and placing it on his thickness. I'd love to drag him into our bedroom right now, but the twins are bounding into the kitchen, looking for breakfast. I groan softly, pulling away from the love of my life.

———

After riding for three glorious days, Ranger and I end up in San Diego. We got a room at a beachside resort, and I smile, thinking my rough and tumble husband doesn't exactly fit in with these men in their hipster clothes and haircuts. Our eyes meet across the lobby and I smile as he walks toward me in his leather boots and blue jeans.

We get an ocean view room, and when we walk into it, we ooh and ahh over the big bathtub, the balcony, the champagne on ice waiting for us.

"It's so romantic," I say, meeting Ranger on the balcony, handing him a glass of champagne.

"To five years of happiness," he says.

"To many more," I add. We drink our champagne, holding onto one another, watching as the sun sets. Tears fill my eyes and Ranger notices.

"What are you thinking about?" he asks, his arm tight around my waist.

"Just thinking about the things we've gone through in the last five years. Lydia growing up, for starters — her life is taking shape in a way we never would have dreamed."

"Roxanne and Stella, too," Ranger adds. Their unlikely love stories reminded us how precious love is, how finding it can change everything. How once you have it in your hands, you should never let go.

"And T-Bone," I say, missing the man who I came to see as a grandpa in the kitchen. We spent a lot of time together flipping flapjacks and making Sunday dinner for Heartland MC. Before he got sick, before we had to say goodbye.

"He was a good man," Ranger says. "Remember when you made him that birthday cake and got two strippers to jump out of it?"

I laugh, remembering the day so vividly. T-Bone was so caught off-guard, but rumor has it, he had a great night.

"The twins learning to walk. Talk. Being their dad has been..." Ranger pulls me to him. "We're lucky Ruby. So damn lucky."

"Do you want to go swimming?" I ask him.

"It's really dark out."

I smile. "Then we can go skinny dipping."

I remember the first time we went skinny dipping, out at Hollow Lake. "No fighting this time though," Ranger says.

Hand in hand, we leave the room and head to the

beach, grabbing towels on our way. We keep walking, past the resort to a more remote stretch where no one is out.

The stars shine and we undress quickly, running into the warm water, shaking with laughter. I gasp, "Phosphorescence!"

It's beautiful. When we push our hands through the water, there is a trail of sparkles left behind. We laugh, moving our bodies, watching the magic unfold.

"God, this is incredible," Ranger says, pulling me close. We are in shallow enough water that we can touch the sandy floor. I wrap my legs around my husband, my arms tight around his neck. His cock is hard, and I lick my lips, relishing how romantic this is.

"You are incredible," I tell him, taking his length in my hand, and sinking down on him, my body filling up with him as he leans down and kisses me.

My eyes close as the moon hangs heavy in the dark sky above us. I ease my hips in gentle circles, refusing to forget a single second of this.

The night I met Ranger, I longed for an ocean, wanting so badly to get swept away in a tide that would carry me away somewhere safe.

Ranger gave me his helmet and I held onto him as we rode though the rainstorm. I clung to him, wondering if he was my ocean, both my deep-sea dive and my life raft.

Now, as we make love with the glittering sea life around us, I open my eyes, looking up at the stars, knowing even if I had a million wishes to make on each of them, I could never wish for something more beautiful than what I already have.

Ranger is more than my ocean.

He is my home.

———

The End

most possessive, devoted, and territorial men *in the country when it comes to the ones they love.*

Heartlands is a rough and rugged new series of standalone stories.

Written by four of the most trusted names in short and steamy romance, each book will get your motors revved and your hearts racing. Guaranteed.

XO, Frankie, Dani, Olivia, and Hope

DOWNLOAD NOW: Heartlands MC Series

ABOUT THE AUTHOR

Frankie Love writes filthy-sweet stories about bad boys
and mountain men.
As a thirty-something mom who is ridiculously in love
with her own bearded hottie, she believes in love-at-
first-sight and happily-ever-afters.
She also believes in the power of a quickie.

Find Frankie here:
www.frankielove.net